The Red Triangle: Being Some Further Chronicles of Martin Hewitt, Investigator

Arthur Morrison

The Red Triangle

BEING SOME FURTHER CHRONICLES OF MARTIN HEWITT,
INVESTIGATOR

By Arthur Morrison

1903

CONTENTS

THE AFFAIR OF SAMUEL'S DIAMONDS

I

I have already recorded many of the adventures of my friend Martin Hewitt, but among them there have been more of a certain few which were discovered to be related together in a very extraordinary manner; and it is to these that I am now at liberty to address myself. There may have been others—cases which gave no indication of their connection with these; some of them indeed I may have told without a suspicion of their connection with the Red Triangle; but the first in which that singular accompaniment became apparent was the matter of Samuel's diamonds. The case exhibited many interesting features, and I was very anxious to report it, with perhaps even less delay than I had thought judicious in other cases; but Hewitt restrained me.

"No, Brett," he said, "there is more to come of this. This particular case is over, it is true, but there is much behind. I've an idea that I shall see that Red Triangle again. I may, or, of course, I may not; but there is deep work going on—very deep work, and whether we see more of it or not, I must keep prepared. I can't afford to throw a single card upon the table. So, as many notes as you please, Brett, for future reference; but no publication yet—none of your journalism!"

Hewitt was right. It was not so long before we heard more of the Red Triangle, and after that more, though the true connection of some of the cases with the mysterious symbol and the meaning of the symbol itself remained for a time undiscovered. But at last Hewitt was able to unmask the hideous secret, and for ever put an end to the evil influence that gathered about the sign; and now there remains no reason why the full story should not be told.

I have told elsewhere of my first acquaintance with Martin Hewitt, of his pleasant and companionable nature, his ordinary height, his stoutness, his round, smiling face—those characteristics that aided him so well in his business of investigator, so unlike was his appearance and manner to that of the private detective of the ordinary person's imagination. Therefore I need only remind my readers that my bachelor chambers were, during most of my acquaintance with Hewitt, in the old building near the Strand, in which Hewitt's office stood at the top of the first flight of stairs; where the plain ground-glass of the door bore as inscription the single word "Hewitt," and the sharp lad, Kerrett, first received visitors in the outer office.

Next door to this old house, at the time I am to speak of, a much newer building stood, especially built for letting out in offices. It happened that one day as Hewitt left his office for a late lunch, he became aware of a pallid and agitated Jew who was pervading the front door of this adjoining building. The man exhibited every sign of nervous expectancy, staring this way and that up and down the busy street, and once or twice rushing aimlessly half-way up the inner stairs, and as often returning to the door. Apprehension was plain on his pale face, and he was clearly in a state that blinded his attention to the ordinary matters about him, just as happens when a man is in momentary and nervous expectation of some serious event.

Noting these things as he passed, with no more than the observation that was his professional habit, Hewitt proceeded to his lunch. This done with, he returned to his office, perceiving, as he passed the next-door building, that the distracted Jew was no longer visible. It seemed plain that the person or the event he had awaited with such obvious nervousness had arrived and passed; one more of the problems, anxieties or crises that join and unravel moment by moment in the human ant-hill of London, had perhaps closed for good or ill within the past half-hour; perhaps it had only begun.

A message awaited Hewitt at his office—an urgent message. The housekeeper had come in from next door, Kerrett reported, with an urgent request that Mr. Martin Hewitt would go immediately to the offices of Mr. Denson, on the third floor. The housekeeper seemed to know little or nothing of the business, except that a Mr. Samuel was alone in Mr. Denson's office, and had sent the message.

With no delay Hewitt transferred himself to the next-door offices. There the housekeeper, who inhabited a uniform and a glass box opposite the foot of the first flight of stairs, directed Hewitt, with the remark that the gentleman was very impatient and very much upset. "Third floor, sir, second door on the right; name Denson on the door. There's no lift."

"W.F. Denson" was the complete name, followed by the line "Foreign and Commission Agent." This Hewitt read with some little difficulty, for the door was open, and on the threshold stood that same agitated Jew whom Hewitt had seen at the front door.

A little less actively perturbed now, he was nevertheless still nervously pale. "Mr. Martin Hewitt?" he cried, while Hewitt was still only at the head of the stairs. "Is it Mr. Martin Hewitt?"

Hewitt came quietly along the corridor, using eyes and ears as he came. The Jew was a man of middle height, very obviously Jewish, and with a slight accent that hinted a Continental origin.

"I have just received your message," Hewitt said, "and, as you see, I am here with no delay. Is Mr. Denson in?"

"No—good heafens no—I would gif anything if he was, Mr. Hewitt. Come in, do! I haf been robbed—robbed by Denson himself, wit'out a wort of doubt. It is terrible—terrible! Fifteen t'ousant pounds! It ruins me, Mr. Hewitt, ruins me! Unless you can recover it! If you recover it, I will pay—pay—oh, I will pay fery well indeed!"

There was a characteristically sudden moderation of the client's emphasis when he came to the engagement to pay. Hewitt had observed it in other clients, but it did not disturb him.

"First," he said, "you must tell me your difficulty. You say you have been robbed of fifteen thousand pounds— —"

"Tiamonts, Mr. Hewitt—tiamonts! All from the case—here is the case, empty— —"

"Let us be methodical. We will shut the door and sit down." Hewitt pressed his client into a chair and produced his note-book. "It will be better to begin at the beginning. First, I should like to know your name, and a few such particulars as that."

3

"Lewis Samuel, Hatton Garden—150, Hatton Garden—tiamont merchant."

"Yes. And what is your connection with Mr. Denson?"

"Business—just business," Samuel responded. He pronounced it "pishness," and it seemed his favourite word. "Like this; I will tell you. I haf known him some time, and did at first small pishness. He bought a little tiamont and haf it set in pracelet, and he pay—straightforward pishness. Then he bought some very good paste stones, all set in gold, and he pay—quite straightforward pishness. At the same time he says, 'I am pishness man myself, Mr. Samuel,' he says, 'and I like to make a little moneys as well as pay out sometimes. Don't you want any little agencies done? I do all foreign commissions, and I can forwart and receive and clear at dock and custom house. If you send any tiamonts I can consign and insure—very cheapest rates to you, special. If you want brokerage or buy and sell for you, confidential, I can do it with lowest commission. Especially I haf good connection with America. I haf many rich Americans, principals and customers,' he says, 'and often I could do pishness for you when they come over.'"

"By which he meant he might sell them diamonds?" Hewitt queried.

"Just so, Mr. Hewitt—reg'lar pishness. And after that two or three little parcels of tiamonts he bought—for American customers, he says. But he says he can do bigger pishness soon. Ay, so he has—goot heavens, he has! But I tell you. I do also one or two small pishnesses with him, and that is all right—he treat me very well and I pay when it suits. Then he says, 'Samuel,' he says, very friendly now inteet, 'Samuel, could you get a nice large lot of tiamonts for an American customer I expect here soon?' And I say, 'Of course I can.' 'Enough,' he says, 'to fit out a rich man's wife—that is, to pegin. He is not long rich, and he will want more soon—ah, she will make him pay! But to pegin—a good fit-out of tiamonts, eh?'

"I tell him yes, and I offer usual commission. But no, says Denson, he wants no commission; he will make his own profit. That I don't mind so long as I get mine; so I agree to put the tiamonts in at a price. The American, he says, is to come over about a big company deal, and when it is through he will pay well. So last week I pring a peautiful collection all cut but unset, and I wait out in that room while Denson shows them to his customer."

"You mean you let them out of your sight?"

"Yes—that is not so uncommon; reg'lar pishness. You see I was out here—this is the only way out. Denson was in the inner office with the stones and the American. Neither could get out without passing here. And I had done pishness with him alretty."

"Well?"

"You see I wait downstairs with my case—this case—till Denson sends down. He doesn't want me to show—fery natural, you see, in pishness. When I sell to make a profit, perhaps for somebody else, I don't want that somebody to know my customer, else he sells direct and I lose my profit—fery natural. See?"

"Of course, I understand. It's a point of business among you gentlemen to keep your own customers to yourselves. And often, no doubt, diamonds pass through several hands before reaching the eventual customer, leaving a profit in each."

"Always, Mr. Hewitt—always, you might say. Well, you see, Denson sends down that his customer is in, and I come up. Denson comes out from the inner office, takes my case, and I wait in there."

The case which Samuel showed Hewitt was of black leather, perhaps eighteen inches long by a foot wide. The arrangement of the office was simple. In this, the outer room, a small space was partitioned off by means of a ground glass screen, and it was in there that Samuel meant that he had waited.

"Well, he took the case in, and I could hear some sound of talking—but not much, you see, the door being shut. After a time the door opens and I hear Denson say: 'Very well, think over it; but don't be long or you'll lose the chance. Excuse me while I put them back in the safe.' Then he shuts the door and brings the case to me and goes back. But of course I stay till I haf looked very carefully through all the tiamonts, in the different compartments of the case, in case one

5

might haf dropped on the floor, or got changed, you know. That is pishness."

"Just so. And they were all right?"

"All right and same as the list—I know well a tiamont that I haf seen once. So I go away, and afterwards Denson tells me that the American liked much the stones but wouldn't quite come up to price. That, of course, is fery usual pishness. 'But he will rise, Samuel,' Denson says. 'I know him quite well, and them tiamonts is as good as sold with a good profit for me; and a good one for you, too, I bet,' he says. I was putting the lot to him for fifteen t'ousant pounds, and it would have been a nice profit in that for me. And then Denson he chaffs me and he says, 'Ah! Samuel,' he says, 'wasn't you afraid my customer and me would hook it out o' the window with all your stones?' I don't like that sort o' joke in pishness, you see, but I say, 'All right—I wasn't afraid o' that. The window was a mile too high, and besides I could see it from where I was a-sitting.' And so I could, you see, plain enough to see if it was opened."

The ground-glass partition, in fact, cut off a part of the window of the outer office, which, being at an angle with the inner room, gave a side view of the window that lighted that apartment.

"Denson laughed at that," Samuel went on. "'Ha-ha!' says he, 'I never thought of that. Then you could see the American's hat hanging up just by the window—rum hat, ain't it?' And that was quite true, for I had noticed it—a big, grey wideawake, almost white."

Hewitt nodded approvingly. "You are quite right," he said, "to tell me everything you recollect, even of the most trivial sort; the smallest thing may be very valuable. So you took your diamonds away the first time, last week. What next?"

"Well, I came again, just the same, to-day, by appointment. Just the same I sat in that place, and just the same Denson took the case into the inner room. 'He's come to buy this time, I can see,' Denson whispers, and winks. 'But he'll fight hard over the price. We'll see!' and off he goes into the other room. Well, I waited. I waited and I waited a long time. I looked out sideways at the window, and there I see the American's big wideawake hat hanging up just inside the other window, same as last time. So I think they are a long time settling the price, and I wait some more. But it is such a very long time, and I begin to feel uneasy. Of course, I know you cannot sell fifteen t'ousant wort' of tiamonts in five minutes—that is not reasonable pishness. But I could hear nothing at all now—not a sound. And the boy—the boy that came down to call me up—he wasn't come back. But there I could see the big wideawake hat still hanging inside the window, and of course I knew there was only one door out of the inner room, right before me, so it seemed foolish to be uneasy. So I waited longer still, but now it was so late, I thought they should have come out to lunch before this, and then I was fery uneasy—fery uneasy inteet. So I thought I would pretend to be a new caller, and I opened the outer office door and banged it, and walked in very loud and knocked on the boy's table. I thought Denson would come when he heard that, but no—there was not a sound. So I got more uneasy, and I opened the window and leaned out as far as I could, to look in at the other window. There I could see nothing but the big hat and the back of a chair and a bit of the room—empty. So I went and banged the outer door again, and called out, 'Hi! Mr. Denson, you're wanted! Hi! d'y'ear?' and knocked with my umbrella on the inner door; and, Mr. Hewitt—you might have knocked me down with half a feather when I got no answer at all—not a sound! I opened the door, Mr. Hewitt, and there was nobody there—nobody! There was my leather case on the table, open—and empty! Fifteen t'ousant pounds in tiamonts, Mr. Hewitt—it ruins me!"

Hewitt rose, and flung wide the inner office door. "This is certainly the only door," he said, "and that is the only window—quite well in view from where you sat. There is the wideawake hat still hanging there—see, it is quite new; obviously brought for you to look at, it would seem. The door and the window were not used, and the chimney is impossible—register grate. But there was one other way—there."

The inner wall of each of the rooms was the wall of the corridor into which all the offices opened, and this corridor was lighted—and the offices partly ventilated—by a sort of hinged casement or fanlight close up by the ceiling, oblong, and extending the most of the length of each room. Plainly an active man, not too stout, might mount a chair-back, and climb very quietly through the opening. "That's the only way," said Hewitt, pointing.

"Yes," answered Samuel, nodding and rubbing his knuckles together nervously. "I saw it—saw it when it was too late. But who'd have thought o' such a thing beforehand? And the American—either there wasn't an American at all, or he got out the same way. But, anyway, here I am, and the tiamonts are gone, and there is nothing here but the furniture—not worth twenty pound!"

"Well," Hewitt said, "so far, I think I understand, though I may have questions to ask presently. But go on."

"Go on? But there is no more, Mr. Hewitt! Quite enough, don't you think? There is no more—I am robbed!"

"But when you found the empty room, and the case, what did you do? Send for the police?"

The Jew's face clouded slightly. "No, Mr. Hewitt," he said, "not for the police, but for you. Reason plain enough. The police make a great fuss, and they want to arrest the criminal. Quite right—I want to arrest him, and punish him too, plenty. But most I want the tiamonts back, because if not it ruins me. If it was to make choice between two things for me, whether to punish Denson or get my tiamonts, then of course I take the tiamonts, and let Denson go—I cannot be ruined. But with the police, if it is their choice, they catch the thief first, and hold him tight, whether it loses the property or not; the property is only second with them—with me it is first and second, and all. So I take no more risks than I can help, Mr. Hewitt. I have sent for you to get first the stones—afterwards the thief if you can. But first my property; you can perhaps find Denson and make him give it up rather than go to prison. That would be better than having him taken and imprisoned, and perhaps the stones put away safe all the time ready for him when he came out."

"Still, the police can do things that I can't," Hewitt interposed; "stop people leaving or landing at ports, and the like. I think we should see them."

Samuel was anxiously emphatic. "No, Mr. Hewitt," he said, "certainly not the police. There are reasons—no, *not* the police, Mr. Hewitt, at any rate, not till you have tried. I cannot haf the police—just yet."

Martin Hewitt shrugged his shoulders. "Very well," he said, "if those are your instructions, I'll do my best. And so you sent for me at once, as soon as you discovered the loss?"

"Yes, at once."

"Without telling anybody else?"

"I haf tolt nobody."

"Did you look about anywhere for Denson—in the street, or what not?"

"No—what was the good? He was gone; there was time for him to go miles."

"Very good. And speaking of time, let me judge how far he may have gone. How long were you kept waiting?"

"Two hours and a quarter, very near—within five minutes."

"By your watch?"

"Yes—I looked often, to see if it was so long waiting as it seemed."

"Very good. Do you happen to have a piece of Denson's writing about you?"

Samuel looked round him. "There's nothing about here," he said, "but perhaps we can find—oh here—here's a post-card." He took the card from his pocket, and gave it to Hewitt.

"There is nothing else to tell me, then?" queried Hewitt. "Are you sure that you have forgotten nothing that has happened since you

9

first arrived—*nothing at all?*" There was meaning in the emphasis, and a sharp look in Hewitt's eyes.

"No, Mr. Hewitt," Samuel answered, hastily; "there is nothing else I can tell you."

"Then I will think it over at once. You had better go back quietly to your office, and think it over yourself, *in case* you have forgotten something; and I need hardly warn you to keep quiet as to what has passed between us—unless you tell the police. I think I shall take the liberty of a glance over Mr. Denson's office, and since his office boy still stays away, I will lend him my clerk for a little. He will keep his eyes open if any callers come, and his ears too. Wait while I fetch him."

II

It was at this point that my humble part in the case began, for Hewitt hurried first to my rooms.

"Brett," he exclaimed, "are you engaged this afternoon?"

"No—nothing important."

"Will you do me a small favour? I have a rather interesting case. I want a man watched for an hour or so, and I haven't a soul to do it. Kerrett *may* be known, and I *am* known. Besides, there is another job for Kerrett."

Of course, I expressed myself willing to do what I could.

"Capital," replied Hewitt. "Come along—you like these adventures, I know, or I wouldn't have asked you; and you know the dodges in this sort of observation. The man is one Samuel, a Jew, of 150 Hatton Garden, diamond dealer. I'll tell you more afterwards. Kerrett and I are going into the offices next door, and I want you to wait thereabout. Presently I will come downstairs with him and he will go away. An hour or so will be enough, probably."

I followed Hewitt downstairs. He took Kerrett with him and locked his office door. I saw them both disappear within the large new building, and I waited near a convenient postal pillar-box, prepared to seem very busy with a few old letters from my pocket until my man's back was turned.

In a very few minutes Hewitt reappeared, this time with a man—a Jew, obviously—whom I remembered having seen already at the door of that office more than an hour before, as I had passed on the way from the bookseller's at the corner. The man walked briskly up the street, and I, on the opposite side, did the same, a little in the rear.

He turned the corner, and at once slackened his pace and looked about him. He took a peep back along the street he had left, and then hailed a cab.

For a hundred yards or more I was obliged to trot, till I saw another cab drop its fare just ahead, and managed to secure it and give the cabman instructions to follow the cab in front, before it turned a corner. The chase was difficult, for the horse that drew me was a poor one, and half a dozen times I thought I had lost sight of the other cab altogether; but my cabman was better than his animal, and from his high perch he kept the chase in view, turning corners and picking out the cab ahead among a dozen others with surprising certainty. We went across Charing Cross Road by way of Cranborne Street, past Leicester Square, through Coventry Street and up the Quadrant and Regent Street. At Oxford Circus the Jew's cab led us to the left, and along Oxford Street we chased it past Bond Street end. Suddenly my cab pulled up with a jerk, and the driver spoke through the trapdoor. "That fare's getting down, sir," he said, "at the corner o' Duke Street."

I thrust a half-crown up through the hole and sprang out. "'E's crossing the road, sir," the cabman finally reported, and I hurried across the street accordingly.

The man I was watching was strikingly Jewish enough, and easy to distinguish in a crowd. I had almost overtaken him before he had gone a dozen yards up the northern end of Duke Street. He walked on into Manchester Square. There a small, neat brougham, with blinds drawn, was being driven slowly round the central garden. I saw Samuel walk hurriedly up to this brougham, which stopped as he approached. He stepped quickly into the carriage and shut the door behind him. The brougham resumed its slow progress, and I loitered, keeping it in view, though the blinds were drawn so close that it was impossible to guess who might be Samuel's companion, if he had one. I think I have said that when the Jew came to the office door with Hewitt I perceived that he was a man I had seen before that day. I was now convinced that I had also seen that same brougham, at the same time; but of this presently.

The carriage made one slow circuit, and then Samuel got out and shut the door quickly again. I took the precaution of turning my back and letting him overtake and pass me on his way back through Duke Street. At the end of the street he mounted an omnibus going east, and I took another seat in the same vehicle. The rest was uninteresting. He went direct to No. 150 Hatton Garden, and there remained. I read his name on the door-post among a score of others, and after a twenty-minutes' wait I returned to my rooms. I had no doubt that it was the meeting in the brougham that Hewitt wished reported, and I remembered his rule was never to watch a man a moment after the main object was secured.

Hewitt was out, and he did not return till after dusk. Then he came straightway to my rooms.

"Well, Brett," he said, "what's the report? As a matter of fact, Samuel is my client, as I shall explain presently. I don't like spying on a client, as a rule, but I was convinced that he was keeping something back from me, and there was something odd about his whole story. But what did you see?"

I told Hewitt the tale of my pursuit as I have told it here. "I came away," I concluded, "after it seemed that he was settled in his office for a bit. But there is another thing you should know. When he first came out with you I recognised him at once as a man I had seen at that same door a little after two o'clock—say a quarter past."

"Yes?" answered Hewitt. "I saw him there myself a little sooner— something like two, I should say. What was he doing?"

"Well," I replied, "he was doing pretty well what he did in Manchester Square. For as a matter of fact the brougham also was here then—just outside the next-door office. I think I might swear to that same brougham—though of course I didn't notice it so particularly that first time."

Hewitt whistled. "Oh!" he said. "Tell me about this. Did he get into the brougham this time?"

"Yes. He came out of the office door with a black leather case in his hand and a very scared look on his face. And he popped into the brougham, leather case, scared look and all."

"Ho—ho!" said Hewitt, thoughtfully, and whistled again. "A black leather case, eh! Come, come, the plot thickens. And what happened? Did the carriage go off?"

"No; I saw nothing more—shouldn't have noticed so much, in fact, if the whole thing hadn't looked a trifle curious. Nervous, pallid Jew with a black case—as though he thought it was dynamite and might go off at any moment—closed brougham, blinds drawn, Jew skipped in and banged the door, but brougham didn't move; and I fancied— perhaps only fancied—that I saw a woman's black veil inside. But then I turned in here and saw no more."

Hewitt sat thoughtfully silent for a few moments. Then he rose and said, "Come next door, and I'll tell you how we stand. The housekeeper will let us in, and we'll see if you can identify that black case anywhere."

It seemed that Hewitt had by this established a good understanding with the housekeeper next door. "Nobody's been, sir," the man said, as he admitted us and closed the heavy doors. "Office boy not come back, nor nothing."

We went up to Denson's office on the third floor, the door of which the housekeeper opened; and having turned on the electric light, he left us.

"Now, is that anything like the case?" Hewitt asked, when the housekeeper was gone; and he lifted from under the table the very black case I had seen Samuel take into the brougham.

I said that I felt as sure of the case as of the brougham. And then Hewitt told me the whole tale of Samuel and his loss of fifteen thousand pounds' worth of diamonds, just as it appears earlier in this narrative.

"Now, see here," said Hewitt, when he had made me acquainted with his client's tale, "there is something odd about all this. See this post-card which Samuel gave me. It is from Denson, and it makes this morning's appointment. See! 'Be down below at eleven sharp' is the message. He came and he waited just two hours and a quarter, as he tells me, being certain to the time within five minutes. That brings, us to a quarter-past one—the time when he finds he is robbed; and he came downstairs in a very agitated state at a quarter-past one, as I have since ascertained. At two I pass and see him still dancing distractedly on the front steps—certainly very much like a man who has had a serious misfortune, or expects one. At a quarter-past two—that was about it, I think?" (I nodded) "At a quarter-past two you see him, still agitated, diving into the brougham with this black case in his hand; and a little afterward—after all this, mind—he tells me this story of a robbery of diamonds from that very case, and assures me that he sent for me the moment he discovered the loss—that is to say, at a quarter-past one, a positive lie—and has told nobody else. He further assures me that he has told me everything that has happened up to the moment he meets me. Then he goes away—to his office, as he tells me. But you find him posting to Manchester Square in a cab, and there once more plunging into that same mysterious closed brougham. Now why should he do that? He has seen the person in that brougham, presumably, an hour before, and there can be nothing more to communicate, except the result of his interview with me—a thing I warned him to keep to himself. It's odd, isn't it?"

"It is. What can be his motive?"

"I want to know his motive. I object to working for a client who deceives me—indeed, it's unsafe. I may be making myself an accomplice in some criminal scheme. You observe that he never called for the police—a natural impulse in a robbed man. Indeed, he expressly vetoes all communication with the police."

"Of course he gave reasons."

"But the reasons are not good enough. I can't stop a man leaving this country anywhere round the coast except by going to the police."

"Can it be," I suggested, "that Samuel and Denson are working in collusion, and have perhaps insured the stones, and now want your help to make out a case of loss?"

"Scarcely that, I think, for more than one reason. First, it isn't a risk any insurer would take, in the circumstances. Next, the insurer would certainly want to know why the police were not informed at once. But there is more. I have not been idle this while, as you would know. I will tell you some of the things I have ascertained. To begin with, Samuel is known in Hatton Garden only as a dealer on a very small and peddling scale. A dabbler in commissions, in fact, rather than a buyer and seller of diamonds in quantities on his own account. His office is nothing but a desk in a small room he shares with two others—small dealers like himself. When I spoke to the people most likely to know, of his offering fifteen thousand pounds' worth of diamonds on his own account, they laughed. An investment of two or three hundred pounds in stones was about his limit, they said. Now that fact offers fresh suggestions, doesn't it?" Hewitt looked at me significantly.

"You mean," I said after a little consideration, "that Samuel may have been entrusted with the diamonds to sell by the real owner, and has made all these arrangements with Denson to get the gems for themselves and represent them as stolen?"

Hewitt nodded thoughtfully. "There's that possibility," he said. "Though even in that case the owner would certainly want to know why the police had not been told, and I don't know what satisfactory answer Samuel could make. And more, I find that no such robbery has been reported to any of the principal dealers in Hatton Garden to-day; and, so far as I can ascertain, none of them has entrusted Samuel with anything like so large a quantity of diamonds as he talks of—lately, at any rate."

"Isn't it possible that the diamonds are purely imaginary?" I suggested. "Mightn't there be some trick played on that basis? Perhaps a trick on the American customer—if there was one."

Hewitt was thoughtful. "There are many possibilities," he said, "which I must consider. The diamonds may even be stolen property to begin with; that would account for a great deal, though perhaps not all. But the whole thing is so oddly suspicious, that unless my client is willing to let me a great deal further into his confidence to-morrow morning I shall throw up the case."

"Did you direct any inquiries after Denson?"

"Of course; which brings me to the other things I have ascertained. He has not been here long—a few months. I cannot find that he has been doing any particular business all the time with anybody except Samuel. With him, however, he seems to have been very friendly. The housekeeper speaks of them as being 'very thick together.' The rooms are cheaply furnished, as you see. And here is another thing to consider. The housekeeper vows that he never left his glass box at the foot of the stairs from the time Samuel went upstairs first to the time when he came down again, vastly agitated, at a quarter-past one, and sent a message; and during all that time *Denson never passed the box*! And the main door is the only way out."

"But wasn't he there at all?"

"Yes, he was there, certainly, when Samuel came. But note, now. Observe the sequence of things as we know them now. First, there is Denson in his office; I can find nothing of any American visitor, and I am convinced that he is a total fiction, either of Denson's or Samuel and Denson together. Denson is in his office. To him comes Samuel. Neither leaves the place till Samuel comes down at a quarter-past one o'clock. I told you he sent some sort of message. The housekeeper tells me that he called a passing commissionaire and gave him something, though whether it was a telegram or a note he did not see; nor does he know the commissionaire, nor his number— though he could easily be found if it became necessary, no doubt. Samuel sends the message, and waits on the steps, watching, in an agitated manner (as would be natural, perhaps, in a man engaged in an anxious and ticklish piece of illegality) for an hour, when this mysterious brougham appears. He takes this black case into the brougham, and he obviously brings it out again, for here it is. Whatever has happened, he brings it out empty. Then he sends the housekeeper for me. When at length I arrive, Denson has certainly gone, but there was an opportunity for that while the housekeeper was absent on the message to my office—*after* all Samuel's agitation, and after he had carried his case to and from the brougham."

"The whole thing is odd enough, certainly, and suspicious enough. Have you found anything else?"

"Yes. Denson lives, or lived, in a boarding house in Bloomsbury. He has only been there two months, however, and they know practically nothing of him. To-day he came home at an unusual time, letting himself in with his latchkey, and went away at once with a bag, but the accounts of the exact time are contradictory. One servant thought it was before twelve, and another insisted that it was after one. He has not been back."

"And the office boy—can't you get some information out of him?"

"He hasn't been seen since the morning. I expect Denson told him to take a whole holiday. I can't find where he lives, at the moment, but no doubt he will turn up to-morrow. Not that I expect to get much from him. But I shan't bother. Unless Mr. Samuel will answer satisfactorily some very plain questions I shall ask—and I don't expect he will—I shall throw up the commission. He called, by the way, not long ago, but I was out. We shall see him in the morning, I expect."

A look round Denson's office taught me no more than it had taught Hewitt already. There were two small rooms, one inside the other, with ordinary and cheap office furniture. It was quite plain that any man of ordinary activity and size could have got out of the inner room into the corridor by the means which Samuel suggested— through the hinged wall-light, near the ceiling. Hewitt had meddled with nothing—he would do no more till he was satisfied of the *bonâ fides* of his client; certainly he would not commit himself to breaking open desks or cupboards. And so, the time for my attendance at the office approaching—I was working on the *Morning Ph[oe]nix* then, and ten at night saw my work begin—we shut Denson's office, and went away.

III

In the morning I was awakened by an impatient knocking at my bedroom door. Going to bed at two or three I was naturally a late riser, and this was about nine. I scrambled sleepily out of bed, and turned the key. Hewitt was standing in my sitting-room, with a newspaper in his hand.

"Sorry to break your morning sleep, Brett," he said, "but something interesting has happened in regard to that business you helped me with yesterday, and you may like to know. Crawl back into bed if you like."

But I was already in my dressing-gown, and groping for my clothes. "No, no, come in and tell me," I said. "What is it?"

Hewitt sat on the bed. "I'll tell you in due order," he said. "First, I saw Samuel again last night—after you had gone away. You remember I went back to my office; I had a letter or two to write which I had set aside in the afternoon. Well, I wrote the letters, shut up, and went downstairs. I opened the outer door, and there was Samuel, in the act of ringing the housekeeper's bell. He said he was very anxious, and couldn't sleep without coming to hear if I had made any progress; he had called before, but I was out. I half thought of taking him back to my office, but decided that it wasn't worth while. So I walked along to the corner of the Strand, till I got him well under the lights. Then I stopped and talked to him. 'You ask about the progress in your case, Mr. Samuel,' I said. 'Now, I have sometimes met people who seem to consider me a sort of prophet, seer, or diviner. As a matter of fact, I am nothing but a professional investigator, and even if I were possessed of such an amazing genius as I lay no claim to, I could never succeed in a case, nor even make progress in it, if my client started me with false information, or only told me half the truth. More, when I find that such is the state of affairs, and that if I am to succeed I must begin by investigating my client before I proceed with his case, I throw that case up on the instant—invariably. Do you understand that? Now I must tell you that I have made no progress with your case, none; for that very reason.'"

"He protested, of course—vowed he had told me the simple truth, and so forth. I replied by asking him certain definite questions. First, I asked him whose the diamonds were. He repeated that they were his own. To that I simply replied, 'Good evening, Mr. Samuel,' and turned away. He came after me beseechingly, and prevaricated. He said something about another party having an interest, but the matter being confidential. To that I responded by asking him with whom he had communicated before sending for me, and who was the person in the brougham which he had twice entered. That flabbergasted him. He said that he couldn't answer those questions without bringing other parties into the matter, to which I answered that it was just those other parties that I meant to know about, if I were to move a step in the matter. At this he got into a sad state— imploring, actually imploring, me not to desert him. He said he should do something desperate—something terrible—that night if I didn't relieve his mind, and undertake the case. What he meant he'd do I didn't know, of course, but it didn't move me. I said finally that I would deal only with principals, and that until I had the personal instructions of the actual owner of the diamonds, in addition to a complete explanation of the brougham incident, I should do nothing, and I recommended him to go to the police; and with that I left him."

"And you got nothing more from him than that?"

"Nothing more; but it was something, you see. He admitted, to all intents, that the diamonds were not his own. And now see here. I suppose I left him about ten o'clock. Here is a paragraph in one of this morning's newspapers. It is only in the one paper; the matter seems to have occurred rather late for press."

Hewitt gave me the paper in his hand, pointing to the following paragraph:

"HORRIBLE DISCOVERY.—A shocking discovery was made just before midnight last night, near the York column, where a police-constable found the dead body of a man lying on the stone steps. The body, which was fully clothed in the ordinary dress of a labouring man, bore plain marks of strangulation, and it was evident that a brutal murder had been committed. A singular circumstance was the presence of a curious reddish mark upon the forehead, at first taken for a wound, but soon discovered to be a mark apparently drawn or impressed on the skin. At the time of going to press, no arrest had been made, and so far the affair appears a mystery."

"Well," I said, "this certainly seems curious, especially in the matter of the mark on the forehead. But what has it all to do— —"

"To do with Samuel and his diamonds, you mean? I'll tell you. *That dead man is Denson!*"

"Denson?" I exclaimed. "Denson? How?"

"I get it from the housekeeper next door. It seems that when the police came to examine the body they found, among other things— money and a watch, and the like—a piece of an addressed envelope, used to hold a few pins—the pins stuck in and the paper rolled up, you know. There was just enough of it to guess the address by—that of the office next door; and it was the only clue they had. So they came along here at once and knocked up the housekeeper. He went with them and instantly recognised Denson, disguised in labourer's clothes, but Denson, he says, unmistakably."

"And the mark on the forehead?"

"That is very odd. It is an outlined triangle, rather less than an inch along each side. It is quite red, he says, and seems to be done in a greasy, sticky sort of ink or colour."

"Was anything found—the diamonds?"

"No. He says there was money—two or three five-pound notes, I believe, some small change, a watch, keys and so forth; but there's not a word of diamonds."

I paused in my dressing. "Does that mean that the murderer has got them?" I asked. Hewitt pursed his lips and shook his head. "It *may* mean that," he said, "but does it look altogether like it when five-pound notes are left? On the other hand, there is the disguise; the only reason that we know of for that would be that he was bolting with the diamonds. But the really puzzling thing is the mark on the forehead. Why that? Of course, the picturesque and romantic thing to suppose is that it is the mark of some criminal club or society. But criminal associations, such as exist, don't do silly things like that. When criminals rob and murder, they don't go leaving their tracks behind them purposely—they leave nothing that could possibly draw attention to them if they can help it; also, they don't leave five-pound notes. But I'm off to have a look at that mark. Inspector Plummer is in charge of the case—you remember Plummer, don't you, in the Stanway Cameo case, and two or three others? Well, Plummer is an old friend of mine, and not only am I interested in this matter myself, but now that it becomes a case of murder, I must tell the police all I know, merely as a loyal citizen. I've an idea they will want to ask our friend Mr. Samuel some very serious questions."

"Will you go now?"

"Yes, I must waste no more time. You get your breakfast and look out for me, or for a message."

Hewitt was off to Vine Street, and I devoted myself to my toilet and my breakfast, vastly mystified by this tragic turn in a matter already puzzling enough.

It was not a messenger, but Hewitt himself, who came back in less than an hour. "Come," he said, "Plummer is below, and we are going next door, to Denson's office. I've an idea that we may get at something at last. The police are after Samuel hot-foot. They think he should be made sure of in any case without delay; and I must say they have some reason, on the face of it."

We joined Plummer at once—I have already spoken of Plummer in my accounts of several of Hewitt's cases in which I met him—and we all turned into the office next door. There we found a very frightened and bewildered office boy, whom Denson had given a holiday yesterday, after sending him down to Samuel. He had come to his work as usual, only to meet the housekeeper's tale of the murder of his master and the end of his business prospects. He had little or no information to impart. He had only been employed for a month or six weeks, and during that time his work had been practically nothing.

Plummer nodded at this information, and sniffed comprehensively at the office furniture. "I know this sort o' stuff," he said. "This is the way they fit up long firm offices and such. This place was taken for the job, that's plain, by one or both of 'em."

The boy's address was taken, and he was given a final holiday, and asked to send up the housekeeper as he went out. Plummer passed Hewitt a bunch of keys.

The housekeeper entered. "Now, Hutt," said Martin Hewitt, "you were saying yesterday, I think, that the main front door was the only entrance and exit for this building?"

"That's so, sir—the only one as anybody can use, except me."

"Oh! then there *is* another, then?"

"Well, not exactly to say an entrance, sir. There's a small private door at the back into the court behind, but that's only opened to take in coals and such, and I always have the key. This house isn't like yours, sir; you have no back way into the court as we have. It's a convenience, sometimes."

"Ah, I've no doubt. Do you happen to have the key with you?"

"It's on the bunch hanging up in my box, sir. Shall I fetch it?"

"I should like to see it, if you will."

The housekeeper disappeared, and presently returned with a large bunch of keys.

"This is the one, Mr. Hewitt," he explained, lifting it from among the rest.

Hewitt examined it closely, and then placed beside it one from the bunch Plummer had given him. "It seems you're not the only person who ever had a key exactly like that, Hutt," he said. "See here—this was found in Mr. Denson's pocket."

Plummer nodded sagaciously. "All in the plant," he said. "See—it's brand new; clean as a new pin, and file marks still on it."

"Take us to this back door, Hutt," Hewitt pursued. "We'll try this key. Is there a back staircase?"

There *was* a small back staircase, leading to the coal-cellars, and only used by servants. Down this we all went, and on a lower landing we stopped before a small door. Hewitt slipped the key in the lock and turned it. The door opened easily, and there before us was the little courtyard which I think I have mentioned in one of my other narratives—the courtyard with a narrow passage leading into the next street.

Martin Hewitt seemed singularly excited. "See there," he said, "that is how Denson left the building without passing the housekeeper's box! And now I'm going to make another shot. See here. This key on Denson's bunch attracted my attention because of its noticeable newness compared with most of the others. *Most* of the others, I say, because there is one other just as bright—see! This small one. Now, Hutt, do you happen to have a key like that also?"

Hutt turned the key over in his hand and glanced from it to his own bunch. "Why, yes, sir!" he said presently. "Yes, sir! It's the same as the key of the fire-hose cupboards!"

"Does that key fit them all? How many fire-hose cupboards are there?"

"Two on each floor, sir, one at each end, just against the mains. And one key fits the lot."

"Show us the nearest to this door."

A short, narrow passage led to the main ground-floor corridor, where a cupboard lettered "Fire Hose" stood next the main and its fittings. "We have to keep the hose-cupboards locked," the housekeeper explained apologetically, "'cause o' mischievous boys in the offices."

This key fitted as well as the other. A long coil of brown leather hose hung within, and in a corner lay a piece of chamois leather evidently used for polishing the brass fittings. This Hewitt pulled aside, and there beneath it lay another and cleaner piece of chamois leather, neatly folded and tied round with cord. Hewitt snatched it up. He unfastened the cord; he unrolled the leather, which was sewn into a sort of bag or satchel; and when at last he spread wide the mouth of this satchel, light seemed to spring from out of it, for there lay a glittering heap of brilliants!

"What!" cried Plummer, who first got his speech. "Diamonds! Samuel's diamonds!"

"Diamonds, at any rate," replied Hewitt, "whether Samuel's or somebody else's. But they can't have been there long. How often is this cupboard opened?"

"Every Saturday reg'lar, sir," replied the housekeeper; "just to dust it out and see things is right."

"Now, see here!" said Martin Hewitt, "I've had luck in my conjectures as yet, and I'll try again. Here is what I believe has happened. Every word that Samuel told me about the theft of those diamonds was true, except as to their ownership. Denson has planned all along to rob him of as big a collection of diamonds as he could prompt him to get together, and he has played up to this for months. His smaller dealings one way and another were ground-bait. Very artfully he let Samuel take the diamonds safely away once, in order that he should be less watchful and less suspicious the second time. This second time he does the trick exactly as we see. He hangs up the imaginary American's hat, he escapes by the fanlight, and he goes out by the back way to avoid the housekeeper's observation. He has arranged beforehand for this, too. He has seized an opportunity when the housekeeper has been out of his box to get wax impressions of these two keys, and he has made copies of them. And here we come on a curious thing. It is easy enough to understand why he should foresee and get himself a key for the back door, in order to make his escape. But why the key of the hose-cupboard? Why, indeed, should he leave the diamonds behind him at all? It is plain that he meant to come back for them—probably at night. He would have been wholly free from observation in that quiet courtyard, and he could let himself in, get the diamonds, and leave again without exciting the smallest alarm or suspicion. But why take all the trouble? Why not stick to the plunder from the beginning? The plain inference is that he feared somebody or something. He feared being stopped and searched, or he feared being waylaid *sometime during yesterday*. By whom? There's the puzzle, and I can't see the bottom of it, I confess. If I could, perhaps I might know something of last night's murder.

"As to Samuel's prevarications, there is only one explanation that will fit, now that the rest is made clear. He must have been entrusted with these diamonds by a private owner, for sale—secretly. Some lady of conspicuous position in difficulties, probably—perhaps unknown to her husband. Such things occur every day. A common expedient is to sell the stones and have good paste substituted, in the same settings. Samuel would be just the man to carry through a transaction of that sort. That would account for everything. The jewels are *en suite*, cut, but unset—taken from a set of jewellery, and paste substituted. Samuel arranges it all for the lady, finds a customer—Denson—who treats him exactly as he has told us. When he realises the loss Samuel doesn't know what to do. He mustn't call the police, being bound to secrecy on the lady's behalf. He sends her a hasty message, and remains keeping watch by Denson's office. She hurries to him with all possible secrecy, keeping her carriage blinds down; he dashes into the brougham to describe the disaster, taking his case with him in his frantic desire to explain things fully. The lady fears publicity, and won't hear of the police—she instructs him to consult me: and consequently, of course, when I recommend communicating with the police he won't listen to the suggestion. Samuel has arranged with the lady to hurry off and report progress as soon as he has consulted me, and this he does, the lady having appointed Manchester Square for the interview. Perhaps she hints some suspicion of Samuel's honesty—rather natural, perhaps, in the circumstances. That terrifies him more than ever, and leads to his frantic appeals to me when I throw the case up. Come, there's my guess at the facts of the case, and I'll back it with twopence and a bit more. Eh, Plummer?"

"I don't take your bet," answered Plummer. "The thing's plain enough; except the murder. There's something deeper there."

Hewitt became grave. "That's true," he said, "and something I can see no way into, as yet. But come—you take this parcel of diamonds, as representing the law. And here comes one of your men, I think."

We had been approaching the front door during this talk, and now a police constable appeared, and saluted Plummer. "Samuel's just been brought in, sir," he reported. "He's half dead with fright, and he's sent a message to Lady H— — in P— — Square; and he says he wants Mr. Martin Hewitt to come and speak for him."

"Poor Samuel!" Hewitt commented. "Come, we'll go and make him happy. Here are the diamonds, and, those safely accounted for, there's no evidence to connect him with the murder. We'll get him out of the mess as soon as possible."

And so they did. Hewitt's reading of the case was correct to a tittle, as it turned out, and with very little delay Samuel was released. But with the message from the police station, the fat was in the fire as regarded Lady H— —. Her husband necessarily became acquainted with everything, and there was serious domestic trouble.

Samuel was glad enough to get quit of the business with no worse than a bad fright, as may well be supposed. He showed himself most grateful to Hewitt in after times, giving him excellent confidential advice and information more than once in matters connected with the diamond trade. He is still in business, I believe, in a much larger way, and I have no doubt he is the wiser for his experience, and for the lesson which Hewitt did not forget to rub well in: that it is useless and worse to place a confidential matter in the hands of a man of Hewitt's profession, and at the same time withhold particulars of the case, however unessential they may appear to be.

But meantime, on the way to Vine Street I asked Hewitt what led him to suppose that the new key on Denson's bunch fitted a lock in that particular office building.

"Call it a lucky guess, if you like," Hewitt answered; "but as a matter of fact it was prompted by pure common sense. Plummer showed me the things found on the body, and I saw at once that the keys offered the only chance of immediate information. I went through them one by one. There was his latchkey—the key with which he had gone into his lodgings to fetch away the disguise. There was another largish key, equally old—probably the key of his office door. There were other smaller keys, also old—plainly belonging to bags and trunks and drawers and so forth. And then there was the large, perfectly new key. What was that? It was not the key of any bag or drawer, clearly—it was the key of a door—a door with a lever lock. What door? Had Denson some other office? Perhaps he had, but first it was best to begin by trying it on places we were already acquainted with. At once I thought of Denson's disappearance unobserved by the housekeeper. Could this be the key of some private exit from the office building? I resolved to test that conjecture first, and it turned out to be the right one. Being successful so far, of course I turned to the other new key and tried that, as you saw."

"But what of that triangular mark on the man's forehead?"

Martin Hewitt became deeply thoughtful. "That," he said, "is a matter wholly beyond me at present, as indeed is the whole business of the murder. Whether we shall ever know more I can't guess, but the matter is deep—deep and difficult and dark. As to the mark itself, that seems to have been impressed from an engraved stamp of some sort. It is a plain equilateral triangle in red outline, measuring about an inch on each side. It is in a greasy, sticky sort of red ink, which may be smeared, but is very difficult, if not impossible, to rub away. What it means I can't at present conjecture. I have told you my reasons for not thinking it the sign of any gang of criminals. But whose sign is it? Surely not that of some self-constituted punisher of crime? For such a person, with no risk to himself, could have handed Denson over to the police, if he knew of his offence. Can he have been murdered by an accomplice? But he used no accomplice; if one thing is plain in all that story of the stolen diamonds it is that Denson did the thing wholly by himself. Besides, an accomplice would have taken the keys and have gone and secured the diamonds for himself; else why the murder at all? But no keys were taken—nothing was taken, as far as we can tell. And why was the body placed in that conspicuous position? It is pretty certain that the crime cannot have happened where the body was found—somebody must have heard or seen a struggle in such a place as that. As it is, I should say, the body was probably brought quietly to the spot in a cab, or some such conveyance.

"But mystery envelops this crime everywhere. So far as I can see, there is no clue whatever beyond the Red Triangle, which, as yet, I cannot understand. The strangling points to the murder being committed by a powerful man, certainly, and it is a form of crime that may have been perpetrated silently. But beyond that I can see nothing. The apparent motivelessness of the thing makes the mystery all the darker, and the circumstances we are acquainted with, instead of helping us, seem to complicate the puzzle.

"What was it that Denson feared when he left those diamonds behind him, when he might have carried them away? And why should he fear it in daytime and not at night, since it would seem plain that he meant to have returned for the stones at night? Where did he go to disguise himself yesterday—we know it was not in his lodgings—and where has he left the clothes he discarded?"

All these doubts and mysteries were destined to be cleared up, in more or less degree; but it was not till Hewitt and I had witnessed other singular adventures that the answer came to the problem, the real meaning of the Red Triangle was made apparent, and its connection with the theft of Samuel's diamonds grew clear. For indeed the connection proved in the end to be very intimate indeed. Once, a little later, we were allowed to see a shade farther into the mystery, as I shall tell in the proper place; but even then the real secret remained hidden from us till the appointed end.

So ended the case of Samuel's diamonds, so far as concerned Samuel himself and the owner; but the case of the Red Triangle had only begun.

THE CASE OF MR. JACOB MASON

I

The mystery of Denson's death remained a mystery, despite all the police could do. The coroner's jury returned a verdict of "Murder by some person or persons unknown"—which, indeed, was all that could be expected of them; for they had no more before them than the bare fact that the body, disguised in the clothes of a labourer, had been found on the steps near the Duke of York's column, just before midnight, by a police constable. But for the housekeeper's identification, even the name of the victim would have been unknown. The jury certainly wasted some time in idle speculation as to the strange triangular mark found on the forehead, without a speck of evidence to help them; but in the end they returned their verdict, and went home.

But the police knew a little more than the jury, though that little rather confused than helped them. They exercised their judgment at the inquest in withholding all evidence of the theft of diamonds on which the victim had been engaged, the curious particulars of which I have already related. In this they followed their usual course in cases where the evidence withheld could give the jury no help in arriving at their verdict, and at the same time might easily hamper further investigations if revealed. For the theft had been frustrated by Martin Hewitt's exertions, as we have seen, and in any case the thief was now dead and beyond the reach of human punishment. The one matter now remaining for the police was inquiry into the murder of this same thief, and the one object of their exertions the apprehension of the murderer or murderers.

The case, as I have already said, was in the hands of Inspector Plummer, an intelligent officer and an old friend of Hewitt's. A few days' work after the inquest yielded Plummer so little result that he called at Hewitt's office to talk matters over.

"I suppose," Plummer began, "it's no use asking if you've heard anything more of that matter of Denson's murder?"

30

Hewitt shook his head. "I haven't heard a word," he said. "If I had, it would have come on to you at once. But I hope you've had some luck yourself?"

"Not a scrap; time wasted; and the few off-chance clues I tried have led nowhere, so that I'm where I was at the start. The thing is quite the oddest in all my experience. See how we stand. Here's a man, Denson, who has just pulled off one of the cleverest jewel robberies ever attempted. He so arranges it that he walks safely off with fifteen thousand pounds' worth of diamonds, leaving the victim, Samuel, stuck patiently in an office for an hour or two before he even begins to suspect anything is wrong, and *then* unable to set the police after him, for the reasons you discovered. But this Denson doesn't carry the plunder off straightway, as he so easily might have done—he conceals it in the very house where the robbery was committed, taking with him a key by aid of which he may return and get it. Why? As you explained, it was probably because he feared somebody—feared being stopped and searched *on the day of the robbery*—not after, since it was plain he meant to return for his booty at night. Who could this have been, and why did Denson fear him? Mystery number one. Then this Denson is found dead that same night disguised in the clothes of a labourer, in a most conspicuous spot in London—the last place in the world one would expect a murderer to select for depositing his victim's body, for it is evidently *not* the place where the murder was committed. More, on the forehead there is this extraordinary impressed mark of a Red Triangle. Now, what can all that mean? Robbery, perhaps one thinks. But the body isn't robbed! There are three five-pound notes on it, besides a sovereign or two and some small change, a watch and chain, keys and all the rest of it. Then one guesses at the diamonds. Perhaps it was an accomplice in the robbery, who finds that Denson is about to bolt with the whole lot. But if there's one thing plain in this amazing business it is that Denson *had* no accomplice; he did the whole thing alone, as you discovered, and he needed no help. More than that, if this were the work of an accomplice why didn't he get the jewels? There were the keys to his hand and he left them! And would such a person actually go out of his way to put the body where it must be discovered at once, instead of concealing it till he could himself get away with the diamonds? Of course not. But there was no accomplice, and it's useless to labour that farther. All these arguments apply equally against the theory that it was the work of some criminal gang. They would have taken all they could get, notes, keys, diamonds and all, and they wouldn't have been so foolish as to exhibit the body with that extraordinary mark; criminal gangs are not such fools as to take unnecessary chances and gratuitously leave tracks behind them, as you know well enough. Well then, there we stand. So far, do you see any more in it than I do?"

Hewitt shook his head. "No," he said, "I can't say I do. All the considerations you have mentioned have already occurred to me. I talked them over, in fact, with my friend Brett. My connection with the case ceased, of course, with the discovery of the jewels, and about the murder I know no more than has been told me. I never saw the body, and so had no opportunity of picking up any overlooked clue; though doubtless you have seen to that. I know not a tittle more than you have just summarised, and on that alone the thing seems mystery pure and unadulterated."

"All there is beyond that was ascertained by the divisional surgeon on examination of the body. The man died from strangulation, as you know, and the natural presumption from that was that the murderer must have been a powerful man. But the surgeon is of the positive opinion—he is certain, in fact—that Denson was strangled with an instrument—a tourniquet."

"A tourniquet?"

"Yes, a surgeon's tourniquet, such as is used to compress a leg or arm and so stop a flow of blood. He considers the marks unmistakable. Now that might point to the murderer being a medical man."

"Conjecturally, yes; though, of course, it justifies nothing more than conjecture."

"Precisely. Well, that was something, but precious little. A tourniquet is a common thing enough—no more than a band with screw fittings, and there was nothing to show that the tourniquet used was any different from a thousand others; and I can see no particular reason why a doctor should commit a murder like this any more than any other man; in which the divisional surgeon agreed with me. And doctor or none, that Red Triangle was altogether unaccounted for. About that, too, by the way, the divisional surgeon told me a little, but a very useless little. The mark was not properly dried, owing to its slightly greasy nature, and although it was almost impossible to remove it wholly, it *was* possible to scrape off a little of the ink, or colour. Here is a little of it on a paper—quite dried now, of course."

Plummer carefully took from his pocket a small folded paper, unfolded it, and revealed a smaller paper within. On this were two little smears of a bright red colour. "There—that's the stuff," he said. "The surgeon examined it, and he reports it to be rather oddly constituted—so as to bear some affinity of meaning, possibly, to the triangle. For the stuff is a compound of three substances—animal, vegetable and mineral; there is a fine vegetable oil, he says, some waxy preparation, certainly of animal origin, and a mineral—cinnabar: vermilion, in fact. But though there *may* be some connection between the triangle and the substances representing the three natural kingdoms, it gives nothing practical—nothing to go on."

Martin Hewitt had been closely examining the marks on the paper, and now he answered, "I'm not so sure of that, though, Plummer. I think at least that it gives us another conjecture. I should guess that the man you want, as well as being acquainted with the use of the tourniquet, has at some time travelled in, or to, China."

"Why?"

"Unless I am wider of the mark than usual, this is the pigment used on Chinese seals. A Chinaman's seal acts for his signature on all sorts of documents; it is impressed or printed by hand pressure from a little engraved stone die, precisely as this triangle seems to have been, and the ink or colour is almost always red, compounded of vermilion, wax, and oil of sesamum."

Plummer sat up with a whistle. "Phew! Then it may have been done by a Chinaman!"

Hewitt shrugged his shoulders. "It's possible," he said; "of course, though, the sign, the triangle, is not a Chinese character. As a character, of course it is the Greek *Delta*. But it may be no character at all. In the signs of the ancient Cabala, the triangle, apex upward as it was in this case, was the symbol of fire; apex downward, it signified water."

Plummer patted the side of his head distractedly. "Heavens!" he said, "don't tell me I'm to search all China, and Greece, and— wherever the cabalistic pundits come from!"

"Well, no," Hewitt answered with a smile. "I think I should, at any rate, begin in this country. I rather think you might make a beginning at Denson. That is what I should do if the case were mine. See if anything can be ascertained of his previous life—probably under another name or names. *He* may have been in China. Yes, certainly, as we stand at present, I should begin at Denson."

"I think I will," the inspector replied, "though there's precious little to begin on there. I'd like to have you with me on this job, but, of course, that's impossible, since it's purely a police matter. But something, some information, may come your way, and in that case you'll let me know at once, of course."

"Of course I shall—it's a serious matter, as well as a strange one. I wish you all luck!"

Plummer departed to grapple with his difficulties, but in fact it was Hewitt who first heard fresh news of the Red Triangle, and that from a wholly unexpected quarter.

It was, indeed, only two days after Plummer's visit that Kerrett brought into Hewitt's private room the card of the Rev. James Potswood, with a request for a consultation. Mr. Potswood's name was known to Hewitt, as, indeed, it was to many people, as that of a most devoted clergyman, rector of a large parish in north-west London, who devoted not only all his time and personal strength to his work, but also spent every penny of his private income on his parish. It was not a small income that Mr. Potswood spent in this unselfish way, for he came of a wealthy family, and though a good part of his parish was inhabited by well-to-do people, there was quite enough poverty and distress in the poorer quarters to cause this excellent man often to regret that his resources were not even larger. He was a spare active grey-whiskered man of nearly sixty, with prominent and not very handsome features, though his face was full of frank and simple kindliness.

"My errand, Mr. Hewitt," he said, "is of a rather vague, not to say visionary, character, and I doubt if you can help me. But at any rate I will explain the trouble as well as I can. In the first place, am I right in supposing that you were in some way professionally engaged in connection with that extraordinary case of murder a week or so ago—the case in which a man named Denson was found dead on the steps by the Duke of York's column?"

"Yes—and no," Hewitt answered. "I was professionally engaged on a certain matter about which you will not wish me to particularise—since it is the business of a client—and in course of it I came upon the other affair."

"Then before I ask what you know of that mysterious event, Mr. Hewitt, I will tell you my story, so that you may judge whether you are able to reveal anything, or to do anything. Of course, what I say is in the strictest confidence."

"Of course."

"I have a parishioner, a Mr. Jacob Mason, of whom I have seen very little of late years—scarcely anything at all, in fact, till a few days ago. He is fairly well to do, I believe, living a somewhat retired life in a house not far from my rectory. For many years he has laboured at natural science—chemistry in particular—and he has a very excellently fitted laboratory attached to his house. He is a widower, with no children of his own, but his orphan niece, a Miss Creswick, lives under his guardianship. Mr. Mason was never a very regular church-goer, but years ago I saw much more of him than I have of late. I must be perfectly frank with you, Mr. Hewitt, if you are to help me, and therefore I must tell you that we disagreed on points of religion, in such a way that I found it difficult to maintain my former regard for Mr. Mason. He had a curiously fantastic mind, and he was constantly being led to tamper with things that I think are best left alone—what is called spiritualism, for instance, and that horrible form of modern superstition which we hear whispers of at times from the Continent—the alleged devil-propitiation or worship. It was not that he did anything I thought morally wrong, you understand—except that he dabbled. And he was always running after some new thing—animal magnetism, or telepathy, or crystal-gazing, or theosophy, or some one of the score of such things that have an attraction for a mind of that sort. And it was a characteristic of each new enthusiasm with him that it prompted him to try to convert *me*; and that in such terms—terms often applied to the doctrines of that religion of which I am a humble minister—as I could in nowise permit in my presence. So that our friendly intercourse, though not interrupted by any definite breaking off, fell away to almost nothing. For which reason I was a little surprised to receive a visit from Mr. Mason on the afternoon of the day on which the newspapers printed the report of the finding of the body of Denson. You may remember that only one morning paper mentioned the matter, and that very briefly; but there were full reports in all the evening papers."

"Yes, the discovery was made very late the previous night."

"So I gathered. Well, I was told that Mr. Mason had been shown into my study, and there I found him. He was in an extremely nervous and agitated state, and he had an evening paper in his hand. With scarcely a preliminary word he burst out, 'Have you seen this in the paper? This—this murder? There—there's the report.' And he thrust the paper into my hands.

"I had not seen or heard anything of the matter, in fact, till that moment, and now he gave me little leisure to read the report. He walked up and down the room, nervously clasping his hands, sometimes together, sometimes at his sides, sometimes before him, shaking his head in a shuddering sort of way, and bursting out once or twice as though the words were uncontrollable, 'What ought I to do? What *can* I do?'

"I looked up from the paper, and he went on, 'Have you read it? It's a murder—a horrid murder. The poor wretched fellow was trying to escape, but he couldn't. It's a murder!'

"'It certainly seems so,' I said. 'But what—did you know this man, Denson?'

"'No, of course not,' Mason replied, 'but there it is, plain enough, and here's another paper with just the same report, but a little shorter.' He pulled the second paper from his pocket. 'I got what different papers I could, but these are the two fullest. It's plain enough it's a brutal murder, isn't it? And the man was a merchant, or an agent, or something, in Portsmouth Street, but he was found in labourer's clothes—proof that he feared it and was trying to escape it; but he couldn't—he couldn't—no! nor anybody. It's awful, awful!'

"'But I don't understand,' I said. 'Won't you sit down?' For Mason continued to pace distractedly about the room. 'What is it you think this unfortunate man was trying to escape? And what am I to do in the matter?'

"He stopped, pressed both hands to his head, and seemed to control himself by a great effort. 'You must excuse me,' he said. 'I'm a bit run down lately, and my nerves are all wrong. I'm talking rather wildly, I'm afraid. I really hardly know why I came to you, except that I haven't a soul I can talk to about—well, about anything, scarcely.'

"He took a chair, and sat for a little while with his head forward on his hand and his eyes directed towards the floor. Then he said, in a musing way, rather as though he was thinking aloud than talking to me, 'You were right, after all, Potswood, and I was a fool to disregard your warnings. I oughtn't to have dabbled—I should have left those things alone.'

"I said nothing, thinking it best not to disturb him, but to leave him free to say what he wanted to say in his own way. He remained quiet for a minute or two more, and then sat up with an appearance of much greater composure. 'You mustn't mind me, Potswood,' he said. 'As I've told you, I'm in a bad state of nerves, and at best I'm an impulsive sort of person, as you know. I needn't have bothered you like this—I came rushing round here without thinking, and if the house had been a bit farther off I should have come to my senses before I reached you. After all, there's nothing so much to disturb one's-self about, and this man—this Denson—may very well have deserved his fate. Don't you think that likely?'

"He added this last question with an involuntary eagerness that scarcely accorded with the indifferent tone with which he had begun. I answered guardedly. I said of course nobody could say what the unhappy man's sins might have been, but that whatever they were they could never justify the fearful sin of murder. 'And,' I added, 'if you know anything of the matter, Mason, or have the smallest suspicion as to who is the guilty person, I'm sure you won't hesitate in your duty.'

"'My duty?' he said. 'Oh yes, of course; my duty. You mean, of course, that any law-abiding citizen who knows of evidence should bring it out. Just so. Of course *I* haven't any evidence—that paper gave me the first news of the thing.'

"'I think,' I rejoined, 'that anybody who was possessed of even less than evidence—of any suspicion which might lead to evidence—should go at once and place the authorities in possession of all he knows or suspects.'

"'Yes,' he said—very calmly now, though it seemed at cost of a great effort—'so he should; so he should, no doubt, in any ordinary case. But sometimes there are difficulties, you know—great difficulties.' He stopped and looked at me furtively and uneasily. 'A man might fear for his own safety—he might even know that to say what he knew would be to condemn himself to sudden death; and more, perhaps, more. Suppose—it might be, you know—suppose, for instance, a man was placed between the alternatives of neglecting this duty and of breaking a—well an oath, a binding oath of a very serious—terrible—character? An oath, we will say, made previously, without any foreknowledge of the crime?'

"I said that any such oath taken without foreknowledge of the crime could not have contemplated such an event, and that however wrong the taking of such an oath might have been in itself, to assist in concealing such a crime as this murder was infinitely worse—infinitely worse than taking the oath, and infinitely worse than breaking it. Though as to the latter, I repeated that any such engagement made without contemplation or foreknowledge of such a crime would seem to be void in that respect. I went further—much further. I conjured him to make no secret of anything he might know, and not to burden his conscience with complicity—for that was what concealment would amount to—in such a terrible crime. I added some further exhortations which I need not repeat now, and presently his assumed calmness departed utterly, and he became even more agitated than when first he came. He would say nothing further, however, and in the end he went away, saying he would 'think over the matter very seriously.'

"It was quite plain to me that my poor friend was suffering acutely from the burden of some terrible secret, and that in his impulsive way he had rushed to confide in me at the first shock of the news of this murder, and that afterwards his courage had failed him. But I conceived it my duty not to allow such a matter to stand thus. Therefore, giving Mason a few hours for calm consideration, I called on him in the evening. I was told that he was not very well and had gone to bed; he had, however, left a message, in case I should call, to the effect that he would come and see me in the morning. I waited the whole of that next morning and the whole of the afternoon, and saw nothing of him. In the evening urgent parish work took me away, but next morning I called again at Mason's house and saw him. This time he avoided the subject—tried to dodge it, in fact. But I was not to be denied, and the result was another scene of alternate agitation and forced calmness. I will not weary you, Mr. Hewitt, with useless repetition, but I may say that I have seen Mason twice since then without bringing him to any definite resolve. As a matter of fact, I believe that he is restrained from saying anything further by fear—sheer terror. He has even gone so far as to deny absolutely that he knows anything of the matter—and then has contradicted himself a minute afterwards. At last, this morning, I have brought him a degree further. In the last few days I made it my business to acquaint myself, as far as possible, with the exact circumstances of the tragedy, so far as they are known, and in course of my inquiries I saw the housekeeper of the offices next door—the man who identified the body as Denson's. He either could not, or would not, tell me very much, but he *did* say that you had been working in some way in connection with the case, and that you knew as much of it as anybody. That gave me an idea. This morning I told Mason that not only he, but I also had a duty in respect to this matter, and my duty was to see that nothing in connection with such a crime as this should be hushed up on any consideration or for anybody's fancies. I said that if he liked he need tell me no more, but might take *you* into consultation professionally, as your client, allowing me first to see you and to assure you that, consistently with his own safety, he was anxious to further the ends of justice. I said that, as your client, your first duty would be to protect him, that your professional practice would keep your mouth absolutely sealed, and that you already knew a good deal about the crime—perhaps more than he suspected. I protested that this seemed to me the very least he could do, and I warned him that if he refused to do even this, I should have to consider whether it was consistent with my character, as a clergyman and a loyal citizen, any longer to conceal the fact that he was keeping back information that might lead to the apprehension of the murderer. This frightened him, and between the fear of the threat and the fear that you might already know more than he suspected, he authorised me—he was even eager about it—to come and see you; always, of course, under a pledge of strict professional secrecy."

"So far your account is quite clear, Mr. Potswood," Hewitt said. "You have done your best, now I must do mine. You wish me to see Mason at once, no doubt?"

"I arranged to bring you to his house, if you were willing and your engagements permitted, at three this afternoon. Will that do? I have been keeping you, I see—it is past one already. Will you lunch with me at my club?"

"With great pleasure—more especially as I have a few questions to ask as we go along. Is it far?"

"Just at this end of Pall Mall—we will walk, if you like."

"Tell me now," said Hewitt as they went, "anything you know about Mr. Mason's habits, family connections, and so forth, as fully and as minutely as you please. Has he any friends connected with China, for instance?"

"China? Why, no, I think not; except—but I'll tell you all I know. Mr. Mason has no family connections, so far as I am aware—at any rate, in London—except his niece, Miss Creswick. She is within a few months of twenty-one, a charming girl, but horribly shut in, for Mason has almost no visitors. Miss Creswick was his sister's daughter; she lost her mother first and then her father, and was left to the guardianship of her uncle. He was also trustee under the will, and he has, I believe, discretion to keep charge of her property, if he thinks fit, till she reaches the age of twenty-five; though in case of his death she is to inherit in the ordinary way, on coming of age. She is a very dutiful and, indeed, an affectionate niece; though I must say he is scarcely fair to her, keeping her, as he does, so completely secluded from the society of young people of her own age. Mere thoughtlessness, I think; he has had no children of his own, his mind is wholly occupied with his science and his fads, and he makes himself a recluse without a thought of the girl. And that brings me to what I was about to say at first, when you asked me if Mr. Mason had any friends connected with China. There is a young doctor—Lawson is his name—some very distant connection of the family, I think, who had a professional appointment of some sort in Shanghai for a year or two, but who is now in London trying to work up a small practice of his own. If you hadn't mentioned China I shouldn't have thought of him, since he never goes to the house now—or, at any rate, is supposed not to go."

"Doesn't go to the house? And why is that?"

"Well, there was a disagreement. What it was I don't quite know, but in the first place it had some connection with some of Mason's experiments—something which Lawson declined to help him with for professional reasons, or else something he declined to do for Lawson, I don't know which. But the thing went further, for, as a matter of fact, there was something between the young people—Lawson is only twenty-eight—and Mason put an end to that. It had been something like a formal engagement, I think, but in the quarrel—Mason was always quarrelling with somebody when he *had* friends, and that's why he has so few now—in the quarrel things were said that ended in a rupture. Whether young Lawson was fortune-hunting or not I cannot say, but Mason certainly accused him of it, and promised to keep back the girl's money as long as he could. In the meantime Mason declared an end to the engagement, and poor Helen was broken-hearted; for as I have said, she is an affectionate girl, and she hadn't a friend to confide in. But I'm boring you—you don't want to know all these things, surely?"

"On the contrary, I can't possibly know too much, and the particulars can't possibly be too minute. Nine cases out of ten I bring to an issue by means of a triviality. You were saying a little while back that there were almost *no* visitors at Mr. Mason's house; but you said 'almost,' and that means there are some. Who are they?"

"Very occasionally—rarely, in fact—there are one or two members of learned societies with whom he had been in correspondence, or who are old friends. There is a Professor Hutton and a Dr. Burge, I believe; but they don't appear once in six months; and there is Mr. Everard Myatt, who is more frequent. He does not profess to be a great man of science, but he is interested in chemistry as an amateur, and is, I fancy, a sort of disciple of Mason's. He has noticed a sad difference in Mason just lately, and he even called on me yesterday, though I hardly knew him by sight, in the hope that I would back up his urgent suggestion that Mason should go off for a change and a rest. Beyond these I don't think I know of a single visitor. But here we are at the Megatherium."

II

Mr. Jacob Mason's house stood in its own grounds in a quiet suburban road. It was not a very large house, but it straggled about comfortably in the manner of detached houses built in the suburbs at a time when space was less valuable than now, and it consisted of two floors only. The front door was not far from the road, and was clearly visible to passengers who might chance to look through either of the two iron gates that opened one on each end of the semi-circular drive.

All these things Martin Hewitt noticed as the Rev. Mr. Potswood pushed open one of these gates, and the two walked up the drive. The front door stood in a portico, and a French window gave access to the roof of this portico from a bedroom or dressing-room. As Hewitt and his companion approached the house the French window was pushed open, and a man appeared—a middle-aged, slightly stoutish man with a short, grey beard; commonplace enough in himself, but now convulsed with noisy anger, shaking his fists and stamping on the portico-roof.

"Get out!" he shouted. "Don't come near my house again, or I'll have you flung out! Go away and take your friends with you! D'you hear? Go away, sir, and don't come here annoying me! Go! Go at once!"

Mr. Potswood absolutely staggered with amazement. "Why," he gasped, "it's Mason! He's mad—clean mad! Why, Mason, my poor friend, don't you know me?"

"Get out, I say!" cried Mason. "Give me no more of your talk! I won't have you here!" And now Hewitt caught a glimpse of a girl's face at the window behind the man—a pale and handsome face, drawn with anxiety and fear.

Hewitt seized the clergyman quickly by the arm. "Come," he whispered hurriedly, "come away at once. There is a reason for this. Get away at once. If you can answer back angrily, do so, but at any rate, come away."

He hurried back to the gate, half dragging the astounded rector, who was all too honest a soul to be able to counterfeit an anger he did not feel, even if his amazement had not made him speechless. Hewitt closed the gate behind him and said as he walked, "Where is the rectory? We will go there. He may have sent a message while you were out."

Mechanically the rector took the first turning. "But he's mad!" he protested. "Mad, poor fellow! Merciful heavens, Mr. Hewitt, his whole tale must have been a delusion! A mere madman's fancy! Poor fellow! We must go back, Mr. Hewitt—we really must! We can't leave that poor girl there alone with a raving maniac!"

"No," Hewitt insisted, "come to the rectory. That is no madness, Mr. Potswood. Couldn't you see the colour of the man under the eyes, and the shaking of his beard? That was not anger and it was not madness. It was terror, Mr. Potswood—sheer, sick terror! Terror, or some emotion very much like it."

"But, if terror, why that outburst? What does it mean? If it were terror, why not rather welcome our company and help?"

"Don't you see, Mr. Potswood?" answered Hewitt. "Don't you guess? *Mason is watched, and he knows it!* He was acting his anger before unseen eyes—and he knew they were on him!"

"God be merciful to us all," ejaculated the clergyman. "Poor man— poor sinner! What is this unspeakable thing which has him in its clutches? What had he done to give himself over to such a power?"

"We can tell nothing, and guess nothing, as yet," Hewitt answered. "Let us see if he has sent you a message. It seems likely. If he has it may help us. If not—then I think we must do something decisive at once. But don't hurry so! It is hard to restrain one's self, I know, but there may be eyes on us, Mr. Potswood, and we must not seem to be persisting in our errand."

So they went through the quiet streets for the two or three furlongs that seemed so many miles to the good parson. Arrived at the rectory, Mr. Potswood pushed impatiently through the gate, and was hurrying toward the house, when he perceived a bent little old man standing among some shrubs with his own gardener, who was digging.

"There's Mason's gardener!" the rector exclaimed, and went to meet him.

The old man touched his hat, looked sharply towards Hewitt, who was waiting near the rectory door, and then disappeared round a corner of the house, the rector following. In a few seconds Mr. Potswood reappeared, with a slip of paper in his hand. "Here," he said, "see this! The old man was told to give it to nobody but me, and in nobody else's presence. He's been waiting since one o'clock."

Scrawled on the paper, in trembling and straggling letters, were these words:—

"You must not bring Mr. Martin Hewitt to my house this afternoon. I am watched. It is hopeless. Do not desert me. Bring him to-night after dark at eight. I shall want his best skill, and you shall know all. After dark. Come to the back gate in the lane, which will be ajar, and through the conservatory at the side, where my niece will be waiting at eight, after dark. Burn this and do not let it out of your sight first. Send a line by this man to say you will do as I ask, but do not say what it is, for fear of accidents. Send at once. Do come at eight, with Mr. Hewitt."

"We must do as he says," remarked Hewitt. "We know nothing of this matter, and we must be guided till we do. Just write an unsigned note—'All shall be as you request,' or words to that effect, and be sure the man gives it to him. Let him out behind through the churchyard, if possible, and tell him not to go straight from one house to the other. Is he an intelligent man?"

"Yes—uncommonly shrewd, I believe. He says he can't have been followed. He knows several gardeners hereabout, and he seems to have called on each of them on his way—in at the front of the garden and out at the back each time, after a few minutes' conversation. Gipps is rather a cunning old fellow."

"Ah," said Hewitt admiringly, "that's the sort of messenger I often want. I'll give him half a crown for himself and the money to pay for a telegram on his way. He knows nothing essential, of course?"

"No—only that his master is in some sort of trouble, and warned him that he might be followed."

"That is good. I shall telegraph to Detective-Inspector Plummer, of Scotland Yard. All right—I quite understand that all I have heard is confidential. I shall tell Plummer nothing till I may—indeed, as yet I have very little to tell that would help him. But I think it will be well to have the police within call—we may want them at a moment's notice; I have no police powers, you see, and Plummer has the Denson case in hand. I will ask him to be here, at this house, before a quarter to eight, if you will allow me."

And so the telegram went to Plummer, and Hewitt, accepting the rector's invitation to an early dinner before starting on their visit, resigned himself to wait. He did not like the waste of time, as he frankly told Mr. Potswood. He would have preferred to see Mason at once, at any risk, and to take what means he thought necessary without delay. But as it seemed that the risk was to be chiefly Mason's, and as Mason knew all of which both he and the rector were ignorant, Mason must be allowed to choose his own time.

The excellent Mr. Potswood endured agonies of suspense, though he also insisted that Mason's wishes must be observed exactly. "What is it all—what can it be?" he ejaculated again and again. "What dreadful influence can thus compass a man about, here in London, in these times?"

It was autumn, and night fell early. Dinner was over at last, and they had scarcely left the table when Plummer arrived, anxious and eager.

"You'll have to trust me a little, Plummer," Hewitt said, when he had made him known to the rector. "I can tell you nothing now—know nothing, in fact, or very little more than nothing. The fact is,

I'm going to see a man who promises information to me alone, in confidence, as his client, and I don't know how long I may have to keep you in the dark. But this is where the trail lies hot, and I know that's where you want to be. More, if you're wanted suddenly you'll be at hand. You have a man or two with you, I suppose, as I suggested?"

"Three of the best of them. They will follow us up. Is it far?"

"No, close enough. It is a house in a walled garden—not a high wall. We go in at a gate from the lane behind, and I think you should wait at that gate, and put your men at hand. We mustn't go in as a crowd. The rector had better go first, and you and I will follow on the opposite side of the road."

So the procession was formed, and it was still some three minutes short of eight o'clock when Hewitt and Plummer joined the clergyman at the door in the garden wall behind Mason's house. The door was ajar as had been promised in Mason's note. Leaving Plummer on guard without, Martin Hewitt and the rector stepped as silently as possible through the little kitchen garden and across a strip of lawn toward where a dull light illuminated the conservatory, at the right-hand end of the house. The door of the conservatory was ajar also, and this the rector pushed open.

"Miss Creswick!" the rector called, in a loud whisper. "Miss Creswick!" And with that a girl appeared within.

"Oh, Mr. Potswood," she said, "I'm so glad you've come! I can't think what's wrong with poor uncle! I'm afraid he must be going mad! He is terrified at something, and he has been getting worse, till he could hardly speak or walk. Dr. Lawson has been—about an hour ago, and since then uncle has been much quieter, in his study."

They were entering the dimly-lighted drawing-room now. "Dr. Lawson?" queried the rector. "Rather an unusual visitor, isn't he? How long has he been gone?"

Miss Creswick flushed slightly through all her paleness and grief. "I don't know," she said. "He let himself out, I fancy. He said he could not stay long when he came, but I didn't hear him go; I have been upstairs, and the servants are in the kitchen—they say uncle's mad, and I'm really afraid he is!"

They left the drawing-room, and walked along the corridor and the hall to the opposite side of the house, where the study lay. Miss Creswick tapped gently at the door, but there was no answer. She tapped again, louder, and then came the faint sound of a quick step on the carpet, and then a slight scraping noise, as when a door is closed over a carpet it will scarcely pass. "That's the window into the garden," said Miss Creswick. "Why is he going out? Uncle! Uncle Jacob!"

But now the silence was wholly unbroken. Hewitt snatched quickly at the door-handle. "Locked!" he said. "Come—the quickest way into the garden!"

They ran out at the front door, and round toward the study window. It was a French window, exactly at the opposite end of the house to the conservatory, and now the gas-light streamed out through one half of it, which stood curtainless and ajar, while the curtain was drawn across the other half. Hewitt was the least familiar with the place, but he was quickest on his legs, and more seriously alarmed than the others. He reached the window first—and instantly turned and thrust the rector back against Miss Creswick. "Quick! take her away," he said; "we are too late!" and in the same moment, even as Hewitt dashed over the threshold, he snatched a whistle from his pocket, and blew his hardest.

There on the floor lay Mason, his face dreadful and staring and black; tight in his neck was the band of a tourniquet, and fresh and wet on his forehead was the Red Triangle.

Hewitt snatched at the screw of the tourniquet behind the neck, and loosened it as quickly as hands could turn. But it was too late. Too late, the examining surgeon afterwards said, by a quarter of an hour.

Plummer was at the window with his men at his heels even before the tourniquet was half unscrewed.

"Round the wall of the garden," shouted Hewitt, "and whistle up the police! He's only this moment out!"

The house was alive with shouts and screams. The rector came running back, and Hewitt, busy with his useless attempt at restoration, called now for a doctor. People were scampering in the street, and Hewitt left the victim to the care of the rector, and himself joined Plummer, all in fewer seconds than it may be told in.

But Plummer and his men were beaten, for nothing—not so much as a moving shadow—was seen in the garden or about the walls. Worse, the general trampling would obliterate possible tracks. Plummer set a guard of police about the wall, and came in for consultation with Hewitt.

The body was carried into another room, and Hewitt and Plummer began an examination of the study.

"No signs of a struggle," commented Plummer, "and there was no noise, they say. That's very odd."

"From what I have seen and heard to-day," said Hewitt, "it is as I should have expected. I believe the man was almost killed by terror before he was strangled—dazed, stricken dumb, paralysed, deafened by it—everything but blinded, poor wretch. And to have been blinded would have been a mercy."

And then, as they made their examination systematically, calmly and without flurry, Hewitt told the whole tale of his day's adventures, together with all he had heard from the rector. "The man's dead," he said, "and his confidence is at an end. Indeed, I never had it—the case, so far as I am concerned, is over before I have even touched it. I haven't had a chance, Plummer; and the thing is deep and dark, deep and dark. Oh, if only the man had let me come to him in the daylight, spite of all! This might all have been averted.... There has been a close search here, too. See how everything is turned over. But, stay!"

A low fire smouldered in the grate, and on it lay ashes of many burnt papers. Hewitt passed the shovel carefully under these ashes, lifted them out and placed them gently on the table under the light of the gas-pendant.

"I must leave you," said Plummer. "There'll be an inspector here from the station in a moment—he won't interfere with you, and if anybody can get information out of this room it's you. The next thing for me is plain. I must make sure of Dr. Lawson, if he can be found."

"That is quite right, without a doubt," Hewitt responded. "I may find anything or nothing in this room, and, meanwhile, he was the last person known to have been here, and the only visitor, and he was not heard to go out, unless we heard him go when we were outside the study door. More, it was plainly some one familiar with the place who was able to get away so quickly by the window and the garden."

"And his interest in getting rid of Mason, too—the girl of age in a few months, and all obstacles to getting hold of her, and her money, removed. And—and the surgical tourniquet, the Chinese colour and everything!"

"Quite right, you must make sure of him, as you say. You will get his address from the rector. Meanwhile I'll try to begin my little contribution to the case—to begin it as best I can, after all the chances have made it useless."

III

It was after nine when Plummer returned. The rector had just rejoined Hewitt in the study, having left poor Miss Creswick, utterly broken down, in her room, in charge of a scarcely less terrified servant. Plummer tapped, and pushed the study door open.

"That's done clean and sure enough," he said, with professional calmness. "And he's a cool hand, is that Dr. Lawson. But have you found anything more? We shall want all we can get."

"We shall," Hewitt assented, "and we shall find more than we've got now, or I'm grievously mistaken. But tell me first what you've done."

He removed the blotting pad, on which the paper ashes still lay, and very carefully shut it away in a wide drawer where no draught could disturb it; he also shut another drawer which stood open.

"We had no difficulty in finding Dr. Lawson," Plummer began. "We met him, in fact, leaving his surgery. I went back with him into the gas-light, and there put it to him plump. Well, he was staggered, badly. Any man would be, of course. But he pulled himself together wonderfully soon, and the first thing he said was that he was just on his way to Mason's house. I thought at first, of course, that he meant to deny that he had been there already, and I gave him the usual warning about what he said being used in evidence. But he went on, and I've got it all safely noted. He admitted that he had been here, at about seven o'clock or just before, and he said he came because Mr. Mason sent for him. That doesn't seem likely, does it, on the facts as we know them?"

"Why, no," said the rector. "The last time he was here he was ordered out, and I know of no reason why he should have been asked to come to-day. We must ask if anybody was sent."

"I have asked," replied Plummer, "just now, and none of the servants was sent. But Lawson's story is that he *was* sent for and came, though he said he shouldn't say what Mason wanted to see him about till he knew more of the case. Looks as though he hadn't quite got his story ready yet, doesn't it? He had thought over the point about not being seen to go away, though; he said he had let himself out at about half-past seven, being familiar with the ways of the house. And he said that Mason was rather unwell—nervously upset—when he left him, but that was all."

"It's terrible," said the rector, "terrible. It seems impossible to believe it of young Lawson; and yet—and yet!" And then after a pause— "Good heavens!" he burst out again. "Why, I only realise it now! There is the other crime, too! Denson! Two murders! Two—and most certainly by the same hand! Mr. Plummer, I *can't* believe it! Oh, there's more behind, more behind, Mr. Hewitt."

"There *is* more," said Hewitt, "as you will see when I tell you the little I have been able to ascertain. There *is* more behind, though I see little of it yet. First——"

There was a sharp knock at the front door, followed by a ring, muffled in the distant kitchen. Hewitt started up. "Who is this late visitor at this unvisited house?" he said. "If it is the police, well enough. But if anybody else—*anybody*—you may call me Doctor, or anything you please, except Martin Hewitt. Don't forget that!"

There were hurried steps in the hall, a question or two, and the study door was pushed open. Two servants—they would not venture from the kitchen singly this dreadful night—made a confused announcement of "Mr. Myatt," and were instantly pushed aside by Mr. Myatt himself, anxious and agitated.

The late Mr. Mason's closest scientific friend was a palish, black-bearded man, of above middle height, with stooping shoulders and a very quick pair of eyes. There was something about his face that somehow reminded Hewitt of portraits he had seen of John Knox, and yet it was not such a face as his; it seemed oddly unlike in its very likeness.

"What is this dreadful news, Mr. Potswood?" he cried. "I heard people talking in the next street on my way home. Is it true? But the servants have told me so. They say our poor friend—but there has been an arrest, hasn't there?"

The rector nodded gravely.

"And who? Tell me about it, Mr. Potswood—tell me!"

"I think I must see how Miss Creswick is doing," said Hewitt, speaking across to Plummer and making for the door.

"Certainly, doctor, certainly!" answered Plummer with a nod.

Hewitt closed the door behind him, leaving the rector in the full tide of his account of the day's events; but Hewitt's way took him to the kitchen, where the servants were cowering and whispering together, frightened and bewildered.

"Is there any paint or varnish of any sort in the place?" he asked sharply. "Give me anything there is—black, if possible—and a brush, quickly."

"There's—there's Brunswick black, sir, for the stove," said the cook.

"That will do; be quick. Oh, there's Gipps, the gardener! You're just the man I want, Gipps. Come and find me a board or a plank, quick as you please!" And Hewitt pushed the old gardener before him into the garden by the kitchen door.

A quarter of an hour later, Mr. Everard Myatt, having heard all that was to be told of his friend's terrible death and the arrest of Mr. Lawson, turned to go, meeting Hewitt at the study door on his way.

"And how is poor Miss Creswick by now, doctor?" he asked anxiously.

Hewitt shook his head. "No better than you could expect," he said, "but, on the whole, no worse. She mustn't be seen to-night, of course, but, perhaps, if you could call round in the morning with the rector——"

"Of course—of course! Poor girl—and Dr. Lawson suspected, too—what a terrible blow for her! Anything I can do, doctor, of course, as I said to Mr. Potswood—anything I can do I will do as gladly as such sad circumstances permit."

The rector had been coming to the door with Mr. Myatt, but Plummer, catching a sign from Hewitt, restrained him unseen, and Hewitt and the visitor walked into the hall together.

"They have put out the light, it seems," Hewitt said. "I wonder why—unless people from the crowd have been coming into the garden and staring in through the glass panels. I wonder if we can find the door-handle. Yes, here it is. Dark outside, too! Good-night—mind how you go on the steps!"

Mr. Myatt checked and stumbled in the dark porch, and reached quickly downward.

"There's a board standing across the porch," he said.

"A board?" replied Hewitt. "So there is. Let me move it, or it'll upset somebody. Good-night!"

Mr. Myatt strode off into the dark night, and Hewitt, noiselessly lifting the board he had himself placed in position, hastened back to the study.

He swung up the board, all sticky and shiny with Brunswick black, and laid it across a spread newspaper, on the table. There on the top, in the midst of the black varnish, were the prints of all five finger-tips of a hand, where Mr. Myatt had felt for the obstruction in the porch.

Hewitt opened the drawer he had shut a little while back, and took therefrom a sheet of writing-paper. And when, with the lens from his pocket, he began to examine that paper in comparison with the finger-marks on the board, Plummer and the rector could see that there were also two distinct finger-marks on the paper and one faint one—all red. Plummer came to look.

"What's this?" he said. "Was this what you were going to tell us about?"

Hewitt did not reply for a few moments, but continued his examination. Then he rose and turned to Plummer.

"You've still got that piece of paper in your pocket, I suppose," he said, "with the little red smudges of colour put there by the police surgeon?"

"Yes—here it is," and the detective took it from his waistcoat pocket.

"Thanks," said Hewitt. "Now, see here. That is a little of the red stuff taken from the mark on Denson's forehead a week ago, and found to consist of vermilion, oil and wax. You have seen the second impression of that awful mark on the forehead of your poor friend Mason, Mr. Potswood, to-night. This room has been searched for papers before we began, and papers have been burnt. In the search this drawer was opened—containing, as you see, nothing but a supply of new headed note-paper. The note-paper was hastily lifted to see if anything else lay beneath, and here, on the bottom sheet, these finger-marks were left in that same adhesive, freely marking red—a sort of stuff that sticks to and marks whatever it touches. The hand that lifted that paper was the hand that impressed that ghastly mark; and the hand that left its print on this black varnish was Mr. Everard Myatt's! Now compare the two!"

Plummer had snatched the lens, and was narrowly comparing the marks ere Hewitt had well finished speaking.

"They are!" he cried, as the rector bent excitedly over him. "They are the same! See—forefinger and middle finger—the same, every line!"

"I needn't tell you," pursued Hewitt, "certainly I needn't tell Plummer, that that is the most certain and scientific method of identification known. The police know that—and use it. But now there is some more. You saw me take that charred paper from the fire. Sometimes words may be read on charred paper—it depends on the paper and the ink. Most of the cinders were too much broken to yield any information, though we may try again by daylight. But one was suggestive. See it!" Hewitt very carefully pulled out the flat drawer that held the cinders.

"You see," he went on, "that one—this—is different from the rest. It has retained its original form better, and has been less broken, because of being of thicker paper. It is a crumpled envelope. Look at the flap—it has never been closed down. Moreover, on that same flap you may read in embossed letters, still visible, part of the name of this house. Plain inference—this was an envelope intended for a letter never sent, and so crumpled up and dropped into the waste-paper basket. But why should such an apparently unimportant thing as that be carefully brought from the waste-paper basket and burnt? Somebody was anxious that the smallest scrap of paper evidencing a certain correspondence should be destroyed. But look closely at the front of the envelope—the ink shows a rather lighter grey than the paper. The address is incomplete—at any rate, no more than some of the first line and a little of the second is at all visible now; but it is plain that the first line begins with an E. The letters immediately following are not distinct, but next there is a capital M beginning a name which is clearly Myatt or Myall. Now, *that* is why, when Myatt came here, I took the first steps to hand to get an impression of his finger-tips, in order to compare them with the marks on that paper."

"But why," asked the astonished rector, "why did he come back?"

"Nothing but a bold measure to see how things were going—he came as his own spy, that's all. He's a keen and dangerous man. Don't you remember telling me how he called on you yesterday, though you hardly knew him by sight, merely to ask you to persuade Mason to take a holiday? It struck me as a little odd at the time. He was pumping you, Mr. Potswood—he wanted to find what Mason had been saying! And he is not alone—plainly he is not alone, for poor Mason knew they were watching everywhere. But come—this is no time for speculation. Plummer—you must hold him safely—we'll pick up evidence enough when you've got him. I wouldn't leave it, Plummer—I'd take him to-night!"

"You're right—right, as usual, Mr. Hewitt," Plummer agreed. "More especially as the rector was—well, a little incautious in talking to him just now."

"I? What did I say?" Mr. Potswood asked, astonished. "I had no suspicions—how could I have——"

"No, Mr. Potswood," the detective replied, "you had no suspicions, and for that very reason, in the excitement of the narrative, you called Mr. Martin Hewitt by his right name at least twice! And after I had called him 'doctor,' too!" he added regretfully.

"Is that so?" asked Hewitt.

The poor rector was sadly abashed. "But I really wasn't aware of it, Mr. Hewitt!" he protested. "I hardly think I could—but, there, perhaps I did! Of course, if Inspector Plummer remembers it——"

"He'll be off!" exclaimed Hewitt. "With that hint, and finding the black stuff on his hands, he'll smell a rat instantly! Come, Mr. Potswood—you can show us the nearest way to his house, at any rate! Come—we may get him yet!"

But the good rector's slip of the tongue was fatal, and Myatt was not yet to meet the fate that fitted him. The house was not far—less than a mile away. It was a detached house, but quite a small one—smaller than Mason's. Plummer blocked every exit with a man, but his caution was wasted. Myatt was gone.

There was the house and the furniture and two servants, just as it might have been any day in the year when Myatt was out for an hour. But now he was out for good. The police watched and waited all night, and all the next day; they waited and watched for a week, and the house was under observation after that, but Myatt never returned. He had made his plans, it was plain, for just such a flight, whenever the necessity might arise; and when he was assured that danger threatened, he simply vanished in the dark of a London night. Search brought no information—not a scrap of telltale paper lay in Calton Lodge—not a letter, not a line. Though, indeed, the police were to see more of Myatt's work yet—and so was Hewitt.

Dr. Lawson's detention did not last the night out. The unhappy Mason had indeed sent to him, by a chance messenger, having grown desperate in long waiting for the return of Gipps from the rectory. Mason was ready to call in any aid, to recall any of the friendships he had sacrificed in the past. But Lawson was long in coming, having received the note after a long professional round, and when at last he arrived, Mason was a little reassured by the promise of Hewitt's visit. Therefore, he did not tell the doctor so much as he might have done. Nevertheless, he talked wildly and vaguely, so that Dr. Lawson feared some disturbance of his reason. The doctor quieted and soothed him, however, and when he left he promised to return after his consultation hour at the surgery was over. He must have been watched away from the house, and then the blow fell that sealed for ever the lips of Jacob Mason.

Poor Miss Creswick was taken from the old house in which she could no longer remain, and for a few months she stayed at the rectory, tended lovingly by the rector's excellent wife—stayed there, in fact, till her wedding-day, which took place early the next year; so that for her and Dr. Lawson the tragedy ended in happiness, after all.

"God forgive me," cried the rector in the grey of the morning, when it became clear that Myatt had escaped—"God forgive me! Through my stupidity a horrible creature has been set loose in the world to work his diabolical will afresh!"

"Never mind," said Hewitt. "It was not stupidity, Mr. Potswood— nothing but your openness of character. You were not trained to the cunning that we must use in my profession. And there will be more than Myatt to take—he was not alone! It is plain that Mason was found to be wavering in whatever horrible allegiance he had bound himself, and he was watched. No, Myatt was not alone!"

"No, I fear not," replied the clergyman. "I fear not: there is horrible mystery still. The watching and besetting that terrified him so much; the fact that he seems to have yielded up his life without a struggle—

and that with help so near; and the connection—what could it have been?—between Mason and the other victim—Denson. That is a deep mystery indeed! And that horrible sign! Mr. Hewitt, you have done much—but not all!"

"No," replied Martin Hewitt, "not nearly all. It is even doubtful whether or not it will be my lot to come across the thing again; but it will be in the hands of the police. And, after all, we have achieved something. For we know that if Myatt can be captured we shall be at the heart of the mystery."

THE CASE OF THE LEVER KEY

I

In some of the cases which we now know to have been connected with the Red Triangle, there was nothing, in the first place, to show any such association. In some of these cases the connection has become apparent only since the final clearing up of the whole mystery, and with these cases we have no present concern; but in others it revealed itself during the investigation of the case. It was to this second category that the next case belonged—the next at all connectible, that is, after that of the mysterious death of Mr. Jacob Mason and the flight of Everard Myatt.

The case was remarkable in other respects also; first, because in one of its features it had a resemblance to the case of Samuel's diamonds, which first brought the Red Triangle to Hewitt's notice; next, because in its course Hewitt encountered what he declared to be the most ingenious and baffling cryptogram that he had ever seen in the length of his strange experience; and thirdly, because I was the means of placing that cryptogram in his hands, owing to one of those odd chances that arise again and again in real life—are, indeed, so common as to pass almost unregarded—and yet might be thought improbable if offered in the guise of a mere story. Hewitt has often alluded to the curious persistence of such chances in his experience. I think I have elsewhere mentioned a certain police officer's prolonged search after a criminal for whose arrest he held a warrant, ending in the discovery—because of a misdirected call—that the man had been living all the time next door to himself; and I have also told of the other detective inspector, who, being sent in search of a criminal of whom he had but the meagrest and most unsatisfactory particulars, and whom he scarcely hoped ever to run down, actually *fell over* the man as he was leaving the office where he had received his information, in the doorway of which the fellow had stooped to tie his shoe-lace! But, as Hewitt would say, nothing but the exceptional nature of the surrounding circumstances makes these things seem extraordinary. What more ordinary experience, for example, than to meet a friend in some London street—perhaps one friend of the only dozen or so you have among the four millions of people about you? The odds against you two, of all the millions, choosing the one street of the thousands in London to walk down at the same minute of time, would seem incalculable; and yet the chance comes off so often as to be a matter of the most ordinary experience.

On this occasion I was expecting orders from my editor to produce certain articles on the subject of the London hospitals. It will be remembered that the matter was very much in the air a few years ago, and as nothing is professionally more uncomfortable than to be called on suddenly for an accurate and reasonable leading article on a subject one knows nothing about, I wrote to my friend, Barton McCarthy, who is house-surgeon at St. Augustine's, and he replied by an offer to tell me anything I cared to ask if I would call at the hospital.

I set out accordingly some little time after a breakfast even later than ordinary, and called in at Hewitt's office on my way downstairs, to say that I should not be lunching at our usual place that day.

"No," Hewitt answered, "nor shall I, I expect. I'm off to the City, at once. I have an urgent message to go immediately to Kingsley, Bell and Dalton's, in Broad Street, where a big bond robbery has just been discovered. Perhaps I can give you a lift in my cab?"

We hurried off together accordingly. Hewitt knew nothing of the case he had to examine, and so could tell me nothing, beyond the short urgent request that he would come at once, and that the matter involved the loss of bonds to a very large amount; and he dropped me at a convenient spot, whence my walk to the hospital was but a short one.

I saw my friend McCarthy, and bothered him very successfully for nearly an hour, getting all the information I had expected, and more, during a very interesting walk through the great hospital.

"You get some idea in a place like this," said McCarthy, as we came at last into the receiving room for accident cases, "you get some idea, Brett, of the size of this great London machine working about us. You might walk about the streets for a week and never see a serious accident, or even an accident at all, and yet, you see, here they come all day long—a stream of people damaged or killed in the machine."

A decent workman was having a gashed hand dressed and strapped, and a navvy with bandages about his head was being led away by a friend. Nurses and dressers were waiting ready to take their orderly turns at the incoming casualties, and as we looked a more serious case was brought in on an ambulance by two policemen. The patient was a ragged, disreputable-looking fellow of middle age, in grimy and tattered clothes, whose head had been roughly bandaged by the policemen who brought him. He had been knocked down and kicked on the head by a butcher's cart-horse, it seemed, in Moorgate Street, and he was quite insensible. A very short examination showed that the case was nothing trivial, and McCarthy sent me to sit in his private room to wait lunch, while he gave the matter his personal attention.

When he returned he brought a small crumpled envelope in his hand. "That case is put to bed," he said, "still insensible."

"Is it very bad?" I asked.

"Slight fracture of the occipital, and, of course, concussion of the brain—probably contusion, too, I expect we shall find presently. Not so over serious for a healthy man, but I'm afraid he's an old soaker— the sort that crumple up at a touch. Nobody knows him, and there's nothing to identify him in the pockets—a few coppers, an old knife, and so on. So we can't send to tell his friends—unless we bring in your friend Martin Hewitt to trace 'em out, which would come too expensive. Besides," McCarthy added, dropping into a seat before his desk, "if he's got any friends they'll come, sooner or later, when they miss him. This is the only thing he'd got beside what's in the pockets—he'd been sent on a message, probably."

My friend held up the crumpled envelope and took from it a small key. "He'd got this envelope gripped tightly in his hand," he said, "but there was no address on it, so we tore it open in the hope of finding one inside. But there was nothing there but the key. If you were a very promising pupil of your friend Hewitt, I should expect you to take a glance at it and tell us the man's address at once, together with his age, birthplace, when vaccinated, and the residence of his maternal grandmother. But you're not, so I'll let you off."

McCarthy turned the key idly about in his hand and tried it on a lock in his desk. "Stopped up," he remarked, withdrawing it, and peeping into the barrel; "not dirt, either—stopped up with paper! What's that for?"

He took a pin to clear the barrel, and the paper came away quite readily. It was a tight little roll, which the surgeon pulled out into a small strip rather less than three inches long and about half-an-inch broad.

"Hullo!" he exclaimed. "Look here! Here's a job for Martin Hewitt, after all! Figures! What does that mean? And what an amazing place to put them in! A key barrel! By Jove, Brett, this looks like one of your favourite adventures. Somebody sends a key in an envelope, and a row of incomprehensible figures rolled up inside the key. Look at it!"

I took the key and the paper. The key was of a good sort; small, inscribed "Tripp's Patent" on the bow, and it evidently belonged to a superior lever lock. The paper which had come from the barrel was very thin and tough—a kind I have seen used in typewriters. It had been very carefully and closely rolled, and then pushed into the key so that its natural tendency to open out held it tightly within. Written upon it with a fine pen appeared a series of very minute figures, thus:—

9, 8, 14, 4, 20, 18, 5, 9; 15, 19, 20,

0, 3, 9, 8, 5; 3, 23, 0, 0, 5, 13, 14,

19; 19, 20, 0, 0, 0, 0, 6, 1; 5, 20, 0,

0, 0, 0, 3, 22; 1, 15, 0, 0, 0, 0, 18,

5; 1, 8, 20, 11, 18, 9, 5, 20; 12, 5,

23, 14, 14, 1, 1, 20.

"Well," inquired McCarthy, "what do you make of it?"

"Not much as yet," I admitted. "But it's pretty certain it must be a cryptogram or code-writing of some sort; and if that's the case, I *think* I might back myself to read it—with a little time." For I well remembered the case of the "Flitterbat Lancers," and the lesson in cypher-reading which Hewitt then gave me.

"Come," my friend replied, much interested, "let's see how you do it. Meantime we'll get on with our lunch."

I took a pencil and a spare sheet of paper, and I studied those figures all through lunch and for some little time after. It soon became plain that the problem was much more difficult than it looked, and I said so. "At the first glance," I said, "it looked a fairly easy cypher; but as a matter of fact, I don't think it's easy at all. One assumes, of course, that the figures stand for letters, and on that assumption two or three peculiarities are noticeable. First, the highest number written here is 23, so that all the letters indicated, in whatever order they may come, are within the compass of the twenty-six letters of the alphabet. Next, the numbers most frequently repeated, if we except the noughts, are 5 and 20, which occur seven times each. Now, the vowel most frequently occurring in average English writing is e, and you will at once perceive that e is number five in the alphabet, counting from the beginning. More, if we go on counting so, we shall find that 20 is *t*, which is one of the most frequently occurring consonants. This would seem to hint that the cypher is of the very simplest description, consisting of the mere substitution of figures for letters in the exact order of the alphabet. But what, then, of the noughts? What can they mean? More especially when we consider that in three places there are actually four noughts in succession; for, of course, no letter is repeated four times successively in any English word, nor in any foreign word that I can imagine. But let us put down the letters in substitution for the figures, on the supposition that the figures stand for letters in their alphabetical order, leaving the noughts as they are. Then we get this."

I rapidly pencilled the letters on the spare paper, thus:—*i, h, n, d, t, r, e, i; 0, s, t, 0, c, i, h, e; c, w, 0, 0, e, m, n, s; s, t, 0, 0, 0, 0, f, a; e, t, 0, 0, 0, 0, c, v; a, 0, 0, 0, 0, r, e; a, h, t, k, r, i, e, t; l, e, w, n, n, a, a, t.*

"See there," I said. "Now, I can make nothing of that. When I come to examine the comparative frequency of the different letters, I find them much as they might be expected to be in a sentence of normal English, and any change would destroy the proportion. *E* and *t* are the most frequent, and then come *a, n, i, r, s,* and *c*. But as they stand they all mean nothing. It is possible that this may be one of the difficult variable letter cyphers, which Hewitt might read, but I can't. But even then, if the values of the letters change as they would do, they would get out of their normal proportions of frequency; so that a variable letter cypher seems unlikely. And there is another oddity. Look, and you will see that, counting the noughts in, the letters go in groups of eight, with a semi-colon at the end of each group. Now, it is impossible that the message can be a sentence in which every word has exactly eight letters—or, at least, I should think so. It can scarcely be that the semi-colon itself means a letter—it would be singular for one letter to occur with such curious regularity as that. There is no other visible division between the words, nor any single one of the usual aids by which the reader of secret cypher is able to take a hold of his work. No, I'm afraid I must give it up; for the present, at any rate. But I really think it is a thing that would vastly interest Hewitt, if I might show it to him. I suppose I mustn't?"

"Well," McCarthy answered, "perhaps it isn't strictly according to rule, but I think I might venture to lend it to you till to-morrow, if that will do. Indeed, I think, on second thoughts, that I may consider myself quite justified, since it may lead to the man's identification, and it will be a sufficient answer to any inquiry to say that I have shown it to Mr. Martin Hewitt for that purpose. But you'll be careful of it, won't you? Do you want the key, too?"

"I think, if I may, I will take the key and the envelope all together. You can never tell what may or what may not help him, and the three things may hang together, and perhaps explain each other in some mysterious way."

"Very good—here's the whole bag of tricks. It's a queer business altogether, and I must say I feel inquisitive; certainly, if Hewitt can get anything out of those figures I shall be mighty curious to know how he does it. You'll come in again to-morrow, then?"

I promised I would, and walked off with the crumpled envelope, the little key, and the puzzling strip of figures. Since the lesson from Hewitt which I have alluded to, I had often amused myself with cryptogram reading, and I had never found a cypher message in a newspaper "agony-column" the meaning of which I could not get at with a little trouble. But this was something altogether beyond me; and if I have any reader who prides himself on his ability to read secret cypher, I recommend him to try his skill on this one before he reads further.

The circumstances, too, seemed as puzzling as the writing itself. Why, if any person wished to send a note and a key in a closed envelope, should he take the trouble to pack the note inside the key? Why, especially when the note was already written in so baffling a cypher? Whither had this ragged messenger been going with the mysterious package, and who had sent him, and why?

Guessing and musing, I reached home, and found that Hewitt had returned before me. I made my way into his office, and came on him sitting at his desk with a large lens, attentively examining a broken brass padlock.

"Am I bothering you?" I asked. "Are you on the bond robbery, now?"

Martin Hewitt nodded, with a jerk of the hand toward the padlock. "It's a tough job," he said, "and I shall shut myself up presently and think hard over it; just now I can't see my way into it at all. But what have you got there?"

"Never mind," I said, "you're too busy now. I came across something very odd at the hospital, which I thought would interest you—that's all."

"Very well, let me see it. I haven't begun my bout of cogitation yet. Show me."

I put the envelope, the key and the paper on the table before him. Hewitt, with a glance of surprise, picked up the key and examined it. "That's curious," he said, and straightway began fitting the key to the broken padlock on the desk.

"Why, man alive!" he cried, with a sudden burst of excitement, "where did you get this? This—this is the article—the key—the very thing I want!" He sprang to his feet and stared in my face in sheer amazement. "Heavens, Brett, the thing's almost supernatural! I've a broken lever padlock here, and of all things in the world I wanted to find the one key that fitted it; and you calmly walk in and clap down the very thing under my nose! Where did you get it?"

I told him the tale of the man who had been knocked down in Moorgate Street, and I explained exactly how the paper, the key and the envelope were found in relation to each other, and why I had brought them.

"And when was the man knocked over?" Hewitt asked.

"Some time between one and two o'clock, I should say," I replied. "They brought him in well before two, at any rate."

Hewitt stared into vacancy for a moment, thinking hard. Then he said, "Brett, I believe you've saved my reputation—not that it could have suffered much, perhaps, in such a desperate case. But as a fact I had already advised the calling in of the police, and should, perhaps, even have given up the part of the case still left me. But this ought to put me on the proper track. You see, every one of these patent lever locks differs in some slight degree from all the rest, and only its own key will fit it; and here, by this amazing piece of good luck, is the one key for this very lock, and the man who had it is detained in hospital. Come, I'm off to see him. Insensible, you say, when you left?"

"Yes," I answered, "and likely to be so for some time, McCarthy thinks; so you probably won't get much information out of him just yet. But the cypher——"

"I'll examine the cypher as I go along, I think. But I should like to take a look at the man, at any rate, even if he can't tell me anything. Will you give me a note to your friend McCarthy?"

"Of course," I answered, readily, and sat down to scribble the few lines necessary to introduce Hewitt.

When I had finished, Hewitt, who had been examining the cryptogram meanwhile, remarked: "This cypher is something out of the common, Brett. I certainly don't expect to be able to read it in the cab-journey—perhaps not in a week of study. The man who devised this is a man of abilities altogether beyond the average."

"I have had my best try at it," I said, "but it beats me wholly. I brought it purely as a matter of curiosity, to show you; it was the merest chance that I brought the key as well."

"And if you hadn't I should probably have put the cypher aside until the case was over, and so have missed the whole thing. Another lesson never to despise what seem like trifles. If you have studied the cypher you have no doubt observed—but there, we'll talk that over afterwards, and the whole case if you like. I'll go now, and I'll tell you all about the business when time permits."

II

Here is the case of the bond robbery as it had been presented to Martin Hewitt that morning, while I was at St. Augustine's Hospital, and as I learned it from him later. I had been a little puzzled to hear Hewitt say that the case had seemed so desperately hopeless that he advised the calling in of the police, because my experience had rather been that it was Hewitt who was commonly called in — often too late — when the police were beaten, and I had never before heard of a case in which this order of things was reversed. It turned out, however, as will be seen, that in the state of the matter as it first presented itself the only measures that seemed possible were such as it was in the power of the police alone to adopt.

Messrs. Kingsley, Bell, and Dalton were an old-established firm of brokers whose operations were not enormous nor much in the eye of the public, but who carried on a steady and reputable business in a set of offices high up in a great building in Broad Street — a building so large that the notice "Offices to let" was a permanent fixture in the front porch. The firm's clients were chiefly steady-going investors of the old-fashioned sort, who wished to avoid all speculative fireworks, and to deal through a firm whose habits were conformable to their own. The last Kingsley had left the firm and soon afterward died, some few years back, and now the head of the firm was Mr. Robert Stanstead Bell, a gentleman of some sixty years of age. There were a couple of sleeping partners — relations — but the one other active partner was Mr. Clarence Dalton, a young man but recently advanced to partnership, and, it was said, likely to become Mr. Bell's son-in-law whenever the old gentleman's daughter Lilian should be married.

The steady, even round of business to which Kingsley, Bell, and Dalton, and their clerks were accustomed was suddenly interrupted by an appalling loss. It was discovered that bonds were missing from the safe, bonds to the amount of some £25,000; and whence, how, or when they were taken was an utter mystery. It was this loss which had occasioned the urgent message to Hewitt.

When Hewitt reached the spot he was shown at once into an inner office, where Mr. Bell sat waiting. The old gentleman was in a sad state of agitation, and it was with some difficulty that Hewitt got from him a reasonably connected account of the trouble.

"The loss comes at such a time, Mr. Hewitt," the senior partner explained, "that I don't know but it may ruin us utterly, unless my clients' property can be recovered. We have had to pay out heavy sums of late to the representatives of dead or retiring partners, and other circumstances combine with these to make the matter in this way even more terribly serious than the very large amount of the loss would seem to suggest. So I beg you will do what you can."

"That of course," responded Hewitt. "But please tell me, as clearly as you can, the precise circumstances of the case. Where were the bonds taken from?"

"This safe," Mr. Bell answered, turning toward a very large and heavy one, which might almost have been called a small strong room. "They were kept, together with others, in this box, one of several, as you see. The box was fastened, like the rest, with a Tripp's patent lever padlock, the only key of which I kept, together with the key of the safe."

The box indicated was one of ordinary thin sheet iron, japanned black—something like what is called a deed box.

"The padlock has been broken open, I see," Hewitt observed.

"Yes, but I did that myself this morning. It had been blocked up in some way, so that the key wouldn't turn—doubtless in order to cause delay when next the box should come to be opened. As it was I might have desisted and put off opening it till later, but I had a reason for wishing to refer at once to a list which was in the box, and so I decided to break the padlock. It was more difficult than one might expect, with such a small padlock."

"And then you discovered your loss?"

"Then I discovered the loss, Mr. Hewitt, though it was a mere chance even then. For see! All the bonds have not been taken, and those left are placed on the top, while the space below is filled with dummies. I hardly know why I turned them over—for the list was at the top—but I did, and then— —" Mr. Bell finished with a despairing gesture.

"And this was some time this morning?"

"At about half-past eleven."

"And when did you last open the box before that?"

"Ten days ago at least, I should think—and even then the bonds may have been gone, for I only opened it to refer to the same list, and I examined nothing else."

"You say that some bonds are left and others are gone. I presume those taken are such as would be easy to negotiate, and those left are such as would be difficult. Is that the fact?"

"Precisely."

"Then the thief evidently knows the ropes, and altogether the matter would seem awkward. For anything short of ten days, you see, and quite possibly for even a longer time than that, these bonds have been in the undisturbed possession of some person who could easily dispose of them, and would certainly do so without a moment's delay."

Mr. Bell nodded sadly. "Quite true," he said.

"But now tell me a little more. You say you yourself keep the only key of the padlock, as well as the key of the safe. So that you open the safe every morning yourself and close it at night?"

"Just so."

"And do you never entrust the keys to anybody else?"

"The key of the safe is on a separate bunch from the key of the box. This second bunch, with the key of the box, is *always* in my pocket, and not a soul else ever touches it. The other bunch, with the outer key of the safe, I sometimes hand to my partner, or to the head clerk, Mr. Foster, if something is wanted from the safe when I am busy.

Though, as a rule, the safe door is open so long as I am about the place. Nothing but the books can be taken out without the use of other keys for the drawers and boxes, which I keep on the private bunch."

"And would it be possible for anybody—anybody at all, mind—to get at that private bunch of keys in such a way, for instance, as to be able to take a wax impression of the key of that bond-box?"

"No, certainly not," Mr. Bell answered with decision. "Certainly not. At any rate, not in this office," he added.

"Ah, not in this office. Anywhere else?"

"No, nor anywhere else, I should think," the other replied, though this time a little more thoughtfully. "There's only my own family at home and the servants and——"

"Anybody who has access to this room of the office?" Hewitt asked keenly.

Mr. Bell seemed a little startled.

"Why, no," he said, "nobody at home comes to the office—not even a visitor, except, of course, my junior partner, who visits the room pretty frequently."

"Very well. You don't remember ever mislaying the keys temporarily, I suppose, either here or at home?"

"No-o," Mr. Bell replied slowly. "I can't say that I do remember anything of the sort. No—and I believe I should be sure to remember if I had."

"Ah! And when you realised your loss what did you do? Told your partner first, I suppose?"

"No—he doesn't know of the discovery. He went out just before I made it, and I don't expect him in again to-day." But as Mr. Bell spoke there grew plain in his face the pallor of a new fear.

Martin Hewitt observed it, but kept his thoughts to himself. "Well," he said, "you didn't tell your partner. Nor the police?"

"No, Mr. Hewitt. You see, of course, the first thing the police attempt is to catch and punish the thief, and they make the recovery of the property a subsidiary object. But for me, Mr. Hewitt, the recovery of the property, as I have explained, is the one great consideration. Punish the thief by all means, but first save me from ruin, Mr. Hewitt! That is why I sent for you; for that, and because I thought it might be advisable to keep the matter quiet, till you had taken some steps."

"There is something in that consideration, certainly. So you have told nobody of the loss, except me?"

"Nobody but Foster, my head clerk—an old and faithful servant. It was he, in fact, who suggested sending for you. As he put it very forcibly, you can act for *me* and my interests, while the police act for themselves, and—very properly, of course, as police—in the interest of the community."

"Very well. I see you have several clerks in the outer office. Do they ever come into this room?"

"Never, unless they are sent for."

"If you and your partner were out, and one of the clerks came in *without* being sent for, the rest would know it, of course?"

"Certainly."

"I observe three private rooms opening out of this. What are they?"

"This is a sort of extra inner room where I have private interviews with clients—I was in there with a client for half an hour this morning before I discovered the loss. The next is a mere little box of a room where the correspondence clerk sits and works. The other is a larger place—it is shared between my partner, Mr. Clarence Dalton, and the head clerk, Mr. Foster."

"Now let me have your broken padlock—and the key. I see you have forced up the front plate with a screw-driver. I will borrow that screw-driver, if you please, and force it off completely."

Hewitt's client produced a screw-driver from a drawer, and in a very few moments the interior of the little padlock lay uncovered. Hewitt examined the lock attentively for some few minutes, trying the key several times against the levers. Then he stood up and said—

"Mr. Bell, you have made a mistake. This is not your lock at all!"

"Not my lock!" exclaimed the broker. "What do you mean? I tell you it is the lock of that box, and I broke it open myself!"

"Yes," answered Hewitt calmly, "it was on that box, and you broke it open yourself; but all the same it is not your lock. Let me explain. These are very good little padlocks, with an excellent lever action, 'dogged against detent,' as the technical phrase goes; so that only the key properly made for each lock will open it. They are so good, indeed, as locks, that it would be a waste of time to try picking them, when, because of their small size, it is so very easy to break them apart, just as you have done yourself, and just as I could probably have done in half the time, having had rather more experience. Now that is what has been done with *your* lock by the person who has your bonds. But of course a broken lock has one disadvantage as compared with a skilfully picked lock—it shows at the first glance what has happened. In this case, Mr. Bell, *your* lock has been broken and taken away, and the thief, having first provided himself with another padlock of precisely the same make and size, has substituted *that*, locked it with its proper key and so left it!"

"What! Then that was why——"

"That, of course, was why you supposed it to be out of order when you attempted to open it with *your* key. As a matter of fact, it is even now in perfectly good order, except for the damage we have jointly committed with the screw-driver. And now, observe! That lock was shut by another key; if the man that did that is as sharp as I suppose he is, he will have got rid of that key at once. But perhaps he hasn't; and if not, then the man who has that key is the thief. At any rate, the key is the clue we must hunt for. Let us have your clerks in one by one, and look at their keys. Some are out at lunch by this time, probably?"

"No—I said they might be wanted, so kept them. I thought you might prefer to see them before they went out."

"Very well thought of, but perhaps scarcely judicious, on the whole. Because if there *is* a guilty person among them it may give him a hint; and the odds are rather against its being very useful, considering the possibility—even probability—that the bonds and the collateral evidence left here days ago. But we'll look at their keys, by all means, and then they may go to lunch as soon as you please. Let me do the talking, or perhaps you'll start a scare. Send for the nearest clerks first, then the others. As each comes in, mention his name, so that I can hear it. Say, 'Oh, Mr. Brown'—or Jones, or what not—'have you some keys about you?' Don't mention my name, and I will do the rest. Push to the door of the safe, and lock this drawer in the table."

Mr. Bell did as Hewitt directed, and then called the head clerk, Mr. Foster, from his room, with the prescribed inquiry about keys.

"Yes, Mr. Foster," Hewitt added pleasantly, "I'm not sure that the lock is quite in order, but I promised to open it for Mr. Bell, so we'll try."

Mr. Foster, a slim, active old gentleman, grown grey in the firm's service, pulled a bunch of keys from his pocket, and Hewitt scrutinised each narrowly. "No," he said, "I'm afraid none of these will do. Stay," he added suddenly, and turning his back, carried the bunch to the window. "No," he concluded, as he came back to the table and tried one of the keys fruitlessly. "No, I'm afraid none of those will do. Thank you, Mr. Foster. You don't happen to have any more, do you?"

No, Mr. Foster hadn't any more, and he retired to his room. Then Mr. Bell called the correspondence clerk, Mr. Henning. Mr. Henning was a much younger man than the head clerk—twenty-six or so— pale and blue-eyed, with weak whiskers and a straggling moustache.

His keys were just as readily produced as Mr. Foster's, but again Hewitt's examination was unsuccessful. The only other key he had belonged to the typewriter, and *that* did not fit.

Then came Mr. Potter, the book-keeper, round, and tubby, and puffy, and his keys went under inspection in the same way, taking a little longer this time, with two separate dashes to the light of the window. Then there was Mr. Robson, young and spruce, Mr. Clancy, older and less tidy, and four or five more. All the keys were examined, all with the same lack of success, and all the clerks were sent away to take their turns at lunch.

"No," Hewitt reported, as soon as he and Mr. Bell were alone again, "it was certainly none of those keys. Though indeed, my little attempt was desperate at best. A man would be a fool to keep *that* key longer than he needed it, and especially to string it with his others. Still, of course, it is by just such blunders as that that nine criminals out of ten are discovered. And now let me take a good look at that box and its contents."

He lifted the box from the safe to the table, and narrowly scrutinised its exterior, especially about the hasp, where the padlock had been. "Either the thief was an experienced hand," he said, "or he took some steady practice with a few such padlocks as this before setting to work. There are no signs of banging about or slipping of tools anywhere."

"But, of course, banging or anything violent would have been noticed in a place like this," Mr. Bell remarked.

"In office hours, yes," responded Hewitt. "But we mustn't forget that office hours are only seven or eight out of the twenty-four."

"But you don't suspect burglary, do you?"

"I'm afraid, as yet, I've precious little ground for suspecting anything definite," Hewitt answered; "but we must keep awake to every possibility. Now let us see the dummies." He turned them over, and loosened them wherever they were tied. "Yes," he remarked, "quite neatly done. Filled in with ordinary blank foolscap, such as, no doubt, you have in your office—but, then, it is in every other office, too; every stationer has it by the ream. No marks anywhere—no old newspapers, nothing that could give the shadow of a clue." He dropped the last of the papers, and turned to his client. "Mr. Bell," he said, "this thing has been thought out to the last inch. There is something like genius in this robbery—if genius is the capacity for taking pains. My advice to you is to call in the Scotland Yard people at once."

"Do you mean you can do nothing?" asked Mr. Bell despairingly. "Don't tell me that, Mr. Hewitt!"

"No, I don't mean that," Hewitt answered. "I mean that until I have had time to think the thing over very thoroughly I can't tell what I can or ought to do. Meantime, I think the police should know; not because I think they can see farther into the thing than I can—for, indeed, I don't think they can; but simply because the thief is getting a longer start every moment, and the police are armed with powers that are not at my disposal. They can get search warrants, stop people at ports and railway stations, arrest suspects—do a score of things that will be necessary. Send to Scotland Yard and get Detective Inspector Plummer, if he's available—he's as good a man as they have. Tell him that you've engaged me, or, better still, write a note to the Scotland Yard authorities, and let me have it, to send or not as I think best, after I have turned the thing over in my mind. I shall take one good look round this office, and then run back to my rooms for an hour or two's hard consideration of whatever I may see. One or two small things I *have* seen already—though I'd rather not mention them till I've made up my mind how they bear. Matters seem likely to have gone so far that perhaps the regular police course of catching the thief first will be the best plan, if it can be done. Meantime, it will be my business to keep my eye first on the recovery of the bonds. But I think we must have the police, Mr. Bell. Now, I'll take my general look round."

III

After Martin Hewitt had rushed off to St. Augustine's Hospital with the key, the envelope, and the cypher I had brought him, I heard nothing of him till dusk fell—about six. Then I received this telegram:—

"Cypher read. Most interesting case. If you can spare an hour be outside 120 Broad Street at six thirty.—HEWITT."

I had to be at my office between eight and nine, and to keep Hewitt's appointment I should probably have to sacrifice my dinner. But I was particularly curious to know the meaning of that cypher, and just as curious to know how it could be read; and, moreover, I knew that any case that Hewitt called interesting would probably be interesting above the common. So I took my hat and sought a cab.

I was first at the meeting-place—indeed, a little before my time. No. 120 Broad Street was a great new building of offices, most, if not all, closed at this time—a fact indicated by the shutting of one of the halves of the big front door, where a char-woman was sweeping the steps under the board which announced that offices were to be let. I waited nearly a quarter of an hour, and then at last a hansom stopped and deposited Hewitt and another older gentleman before me.

"Hope we haven't kept you waiting, Brett," Hewitt said. "This is Mr. Bell, of Kingsley, Bell and Dalton; it took me a little longer than I expected to reach him. His offices are shut, and the clerks all gone, but we are going to turn up the lights for a bit. The lift man is gone too, I expect, so we shall have a good long stair-climb."

As to the lift man Hewitt was right, and during our long climb I received, briefly, an account of the loss Mr. Bell's firm had suffered. "I have told Mr. Bell," Hewitt said, "that it was you who happened across the key in such an odd fashion, and when I wired I was sure he would be glad to let you see the upshot of your strange bit of luck. I was also pretty sure that you would like to see it, too. For I really believe that this case—which I confess seemed pretty near hopeless a few hours ago—is coming to an issue now, and here."

"Did you get any information out of the man in the hospital?" I asked.

"Not a scrap," Hewitt replied. "He was still insensible, and though I saw his clothes, and they told me a good deal about the gentleman's personal habits—which are not dazzlingly noble, to put it mildly—they told me nothing else whatever, except that he had recently been knocked down in the mud, which I knew already. But the cypher has told me something, as I will explain presently."

By this time we had reached the high floor in which the offices stood, and Mr. Bell, all wonder and pale agitation, unlocked the outer door, and turned on the electric light.

"Now," cried Hewitt, "show me your ventilators!"

There were some, it seemed, in the top panes of the windows, but these were not what Hewitt wanted. There were others in the form of upright chambers or flues, made of metal, and painted the same colour as the walls about them. They rose from the floor in corners and wall angles, and could be shut or opened by means of lids over their upper ends. These were more to Hewitt's mind, and he went about from one to another, groping under the lids, and poking down into the flues with a walking-stick. There was a wire-grating, or diaphragm, it seemed, in each of them, two or three feet down, and we could hear the end of the stick raking on this at each investigation. One after another of these ventilators Hewitt examined, till he had examined them all, in outer and inner rooms, without result; and I could see that he was disappointed.

"There must be another somewhere," he said, and hunted afresh.

But plainly he had tried them all, and now he could do no more than try them all again, with as little result.

"It *is* a ventilator," he said, positively. "Unless——" he broke off thoughtfully and stood silent for a few moments. "Ah! of course!" he resumed presently. "We'll send for the housekeeper and a candle.

Which is the nearest empty office—the nearest office to let? Is there one on this floor?"

"I think not," Mr. Bell answered. "But there's one on the floor below, just opposite the lift—I see the bill on the door every day as I come up."

"We'll try that, then. I'll rake out every ventilator in this palatial edifice before I'll call myself beaten. Come, call the housekeeper. Is there a speaking tube? Tell him to bring a light."

The housekeeper came, wonderingly, with a watch-man's oil-lantern, and we all went to the floor below. Opposite the lift was a glass door from which a bill had recently been torn.

"Why, it's let!" said Mr. Bell.

"Yes, sir," assented the housekeeper. "Let a day or two ago to a Mr. Catherton Hunt. Or, at least, a deposit was paid."

"But see—the door's not locked," Hewitt observed, pushing it open. "I think we'll trespass on Mr. Catherton Hunt's new offices, since they seem quite empty, and he hasn't taken possession. Come—ventilators!"

It was a small office—an outer room of moderate size, and one smaller inner room. Hewitt at once attacked the ventilators in the larger apartment—there were two of them—but retired disappointed from each. There was one ventilator only in the small room. Hewitt tilted the lid, which was at about the level of his eyes, thrust in his hand, and drew forth a bundle of folded papers; thrust in his hand again and drew forth another bundle; did it again, and drew forth more!

Mr. Bell fell upon the first bundle almost as a dog falls upon a bone; and now he snatched eagerly at each successive paper or bundle, till Hewitt raked the grating with his stick, and declared that there were no more. "Is that all?" he asked.

Mr. Bell went tremblingly from paper to paper, and, at last, said that he believed it really was. "I can verify it by the list upstairs," he added, "if you are sure there are no more."

"No more," repeated Hewitt, rattling his stick in the ventilator again. "Let us go and verify, by all means."

We sent the puzzled housekeeper away, and returned to the office above, and presently Mr. Bell, now beginning so far to recover from his amazement as to express incoherent gratitude, reported that the bonds were correct and complete to the last and least.

"Very well," said Hewitt, "then my part of the business is done, though I must say I've had luck, or rather, Brett has had it for me. But the police must come on now. I think, Mr. Bell, we'll go along to Scotland Yard when we leave here. They'll be wanting to see Mr. Catherton Hunt, I expect, whoever he is—and somebody in your office, too, if I'm not sadly mistaken."

"Who?" gasped Mr. Bell.

"That, perhaps, you can help to point out. See here—do you know whose figures they are?" and Hewitt produced the small slip of paper containing the cypher.

"They're very small," remarked Mr. Bell, putting on his glasses; "very small indeed; but I think—why they're Henning's, I do believe!"

"Ah! one or two other little things seemed to point that way. Henning is your correspondence clerk, I believe, and I expect this thin little slip is a specimen of your typewriter paper. Have you any of his written figures for comparison?"

"Well no—I hardly think—you see he typewrites his letters, and although I know his writing very well I can't at the moment put my hand on any figures of his."

"Never mind—it's mere matter of curiosity; the police will ask him questions in the morning. What *I* believe has happened is this. Our friend Henning—if he's the man—has a friend outside a great deal cleverer than himself—though he would seem to have his share of cunning, too. Between them they resolved to rob you in the way they have done—temporarily. Henning was to take advantage of his position in that little inner room to get at the safe some day when it was open and when you were engaged in your own private inner room with a client, so leaving the safe unwatched. He was provided with a spare patent padlock and key, of the sort you used on that black box, and his confederate had drilled him in the trick of breaking that particular sort of padlock open, with other spare specimens. He got his opportunity this morning."

"Only this morning?"

"This morning, I think, else we should never have got these bonds back, nor even have heard of them again. I think you said you were engaged with a client for half an hour?"

"Yes, from about half-past ten to eleven."

"That was his chance, and he took it. He broke the padlock, took out the bonds, substituted the dummies he had already prepared in his own desk, and locked the box again with the new padlock. Meantime Hunt had paid a deposit, pending references, on the office below—the nearest empty room. Of course, he wouldn't get the key until the tenancy was finally accepted—which he never intended it should be. But he easily arranged to have the door left unlocked for a day or two, on some convenient excuse—arranging decorations, or what not. And the bill was taken down, so that prospective and prospecting tenants were kept away. The bonds being stolen, Henning took the first opportunity of carrying them to the empty office—probably piecemeal—a thing he could easily manage almost under your nose, before you were aware of your loss. There he was to conceal them, either in the chimney, under the boards, or in the ventilator, as he might find convenient—and he found the ventilator most convenient. Then he was to apprise his confederate of the fact that the robbery had been effected in order that Hunt might come and quietly fetch the plunder away. The message was to take an ingenious form. Hunt was to have a fellow waiting about in the street, and as soon as Henning could get out—say to lunch—he was just to *send the key* by this messenger—the key with which he had locked the new padlock on the black box. You see the advantages of that simple arrangement. First, the key, which is evidence, is got rid of in a safe and effectual way—a thing that couldn't be done as well by merely flinging it away on or near the premises, where it might be found. Next, the message is perfectly secret—the messenger could never guess what the key meant, nor could any other person not in the confederate's confidence. And, at the same time, the key tells all that is necessary; the robbery has been effected—come and remove the plunder.

"But something unforeseen happens. No sooner are the bonds stolen and safely hidden than you go to the box, find something wrong with the lock, break it open and discover the loss. This was a thing that they trusted would not happen till after the bonds were safely got away. More, I am sent for, the clerks are kept in from lunch, and so on. Henning gets into a funk, and resolves to send a message of special urgency to his confederate. For that purpose he uses a cypher which the two have agreed upon—the most ingenious cypher I have ever seen used for the purpose. He doesn't wish to make his message any more conspicuous than he need, so he writes his cypher on this scrap of paper and rolls it inside the key—probably another expedient agreed upon in case of necessity. Then the key goes into an envelope, for greater security of the cypher message, and the messenger gets it when Henning is at last released for lunch. What happened to the message we know; and here it is.

"Now I will not weary you with a detailed account of the different ways in which I attacked this cypher, but I will take the shortest possible cut to the true interpretation. A very short examination of the cryptogram shows that while no number is included above 23, the numbers, in their relative frequency, roughly agree with the relative frequency of the corresponding letters of the alphabet, *a* for 1, *b* for 2, and so on."

Here I handed Hewitt the pencilled note I had made at the hospital, with letters substituted for the figures, thus:—*i, h, n, d, t, r, e, i; 0, s, t, 0, c, i, h, e; c, w, 0, 0, e, m, n, s; s, t, 0, 0, 0, 0, f, a; e, t, 0, 0, 0, 0, c, v; a, o, 0, 0, 0, 0, r, e; a, h, t, k, r, i, e, t; l, e, w, n, n, a, a, t.*

Hewitt took the paper and went on. "If that were all the thing would be childishly simple. But you will see that we seem as far from the solution as ever; for the letters as they stand mean nothing, though in fact they are in normal relative frequency; so that if they mean other letters, all the rules are upset, and we are at a standstill. I admit that for a long time the thing bothered me. But a peculiarity struck me. Not only were the figures, or letters, disposed in groups of *eight*, but there were also *eight* such groups—sixty-four altogether. What did that suggest? What but a chessboard?"

"A chessboard?" I queried.

"Just so—a chessboard. Eight squares each way—sixty-four altogether. So I drew a rough representation of a chessboard, and set out the letters on it, in their order, like this:—

i	h	n	d	t	r	e	i
o	s	t	o	c	i	h	e
c	w	o	o	e	m	n	s
s	t	o	o	o	o	f	a
e	t	o	o	o	o	c	v
a	o	o	o	o	o	r	e
a	h	t	k	r	i	e	t
l	e	w	n	n	a	a	t

"Now, there was my chessboard with my letters on it. I tried reading them downward, across, upward and diagonally, in the direction of the moves of different chess pieces—king, queen, rook and bishop. Nothing came of that, whatever I did; the thing was as unreadable as ever. But there remained one chess-move to try—the eccentric move of the knight; the move of one square forward, backward or sideways, and then one square diagonally, or, as it has sometimes been more concisely expressed, the move to the next square but one of a different colour from that on which it rests. I tried the knight's move, and I read the cypher.

84

"I began at the top left-hand corner, just as one does in reading a book. I read the moves downward—*i* to *w*, *e* and *h*, and found that led to nothing. So I took the one alternative move, and, with a little consideration, skipped along from *i* to *t* in the second line of squares, *t* in the top line, *h* in the second line, *e* in the third, *r* in the top and *e* in the second. That gave me an idea. There were the letters *i*, *t*, *t*, followed by the word *here*. I tried back from the *i* again, and taking in the reverse order the *w*, *e* and *h* which I had first given up, I read my own name, as you can see it, from the *h* on the bottom line but one, moving upward. So I had the words *Hewitt here*. I need not carry you through all the steps, which will now be plain enough to you. But I found that the message actually began in the *right*-hand corner, and read thus, the noughts counting for nothing—

"'*Invent loss disc take at once Martin Hewitt here fear watch.*'

"The noughts were plainly merely inserted to fill in unneeded squares, and keep the rest of the figures in their proper relative places when the cypher was written in line. At first I was a little puzzled to understand what seemed to be the first word *invent*. But it was quite clear that *loss disc* meant 'loss discovered,' so I concluded that here in the beginning was a contraction also, and that *in* was a separate word. In that case *vent* could be a contraction for no other word but 'ventilator,' in accordance with the sense of the words. So I concluded that the meaning of the whole sentence was simply this: 'The plunder is in the ventilator, the loss is discovered, take away the booty at once; Martin Hewitt is here, and I fear I may be watched.' There is the reading, and our little adventure this evening is what it has led to.

"Of course, the confederate wouldn't go groping about the squares so painfully as I have had to do. To him the reading would be simple enough, for the order of the moves would be preconcerted. Each of the conspirators would have, as a guide, both to reading and writing the cypher, a drawn set of squares, numbered in the order of the moves—1 where we have the *i*, 2 where we have the *n*, 3 where we have the *v*, and so on. With that before him, either reading or writing in this extraordinary cryptogram would be easy and quick enough. And now for Scotland Yard!"

IV

We learned late on the following day that Henning had not appeared at the office. From that we assumed that he must have met his confederate in the evening, and, finding that he had not received the message sent, conceived that something was wrong, and made himself safe. The confederate, Hunt, however, made his appearance early next morning, but escaped.

What happened is best told in Plummer's words when he called on Hewitt in the afternoon.

"I went round this morning," he said, "as I said I would last night. I took a good man with me, and we got the dummy bonds that had been put in Bell's box and popped 'em in the ventilator, where the real ones had been hidden. You see, we'd got nothing *legal* against Catherton Hunt as yet, but if we could only grab him with those dummy bonds on him it might help, with the other evidence we could scrape up (and especially if we could take Henning), to sustain a charge of conspiracy to steal. Well, he came so quick he was on us before we were quite ready. We'd got the dummies in their place, and I was in front of the door telling my man the likeliest corner to wait in, when suddenly up pops the lift right in front of me, with a gentleman in it—clean-shaven. I looked at him and he looked at me. I had a sort of distant notion that I might have seen him before, and it's pretty certain he had something more than a distant notion about me. 'Down again,' he says to the lift man, before the gate was swung, 'I've forgotten something!' And down the lift went. You'll understand I had no idea he was the man we wanted; but as the lift went down and my eyes were on the man's face, I saw who he was! When he stood straight before me I had no more than a vague notion that I'd seen him somewhere before. But down the lift went, and in the flash of time when he'd nearly disappeared, and the bottom part of his face was hidden by the sill of the lift opening—the part of his face where his beard had been when we met him last—I saw it was Myatt!"

"Myatt? Good heavens!"

"Everard Myatt, Mr. Hewitt, the man that murdered Mr. Jacob Mason! Everard Myatt, for a thousand, with his beard shaved! And we've lost him again! What could we do? We shouted and ran downstairs, and that was all. He'd gone, of course. And when we asked the hall porter he told us that Mr. Catherton Hunt had just come down the lift and hurried out!"

THE CASE OF THE BURNT BARN

I

Everard Myatt—or Catherton Hunt—was lost again. Martin Hewitt had been wholly successful, for he had recovered Mr. Bell's missing bonds; but the police caught neither of the conspirators. Investigation at Henning's lodgings showed that careful preparations must have been made for an immediate flight if it should become necessary, and the flight had taken place. The man in the hospital, who had been knocked down in carrying from one to the other the extraordinary message that Hewitt deciphered, remained insensible for a few days, and could not be questioned till some time later still. Then he professed to have forgotten all about the message on which he was going when he met his accident, and the medical men in attendance informed the police that it was quite possible that the fellow's statement was true. He said that he *did* carry messages sometimes, when he could get a job, but he could remember nothing of the message of the key, nor of who had sent him, nor where he was to go. Nevertheless, the police, although they professed to accept his statement, kept a wary eye on him after his discharge from the hospital, for they had a very great suspicion that he knew more than he chose to tell. But nothing more was heard of the accomplices till another case of Martin Hewitt's brought the news, and that in a manner strange enough.

The matter began, as so many matters of Hewitt's did, with the receipt of a telegram, followed immediately by another. For the first having been handed in at a country office not very long before eight the previous evening, it was not delivered at Hewitt's office till the morning, in accordance with the ancient manners and customs observed in the telegraphic system of this country. It had been despatched from Throckham, in Middlesex, and it was simply a very urgently worded request to Hewitt to come at once, signed "Claire Peytral." The second telegram, which came even as Hewitt was reading the first, on his arrival at his office, ran thus:—

"Did you receive telegram? See newspapers. Matter life or death. Would come personally but cannot leave mother. Pray answer.— PEYTRAL."

The answer went instantly that Hewitt would come by the next train, for he had seen the morning paper and from that knew the urgency of the case. But a consultation of the railway guide showed that trains to Throckham were fewer than one might suppose, considering the proximity of the village to London, and that the next would leave in about an hour and a quarter; so that I saw Hewitt before he started. He came up to my rooms, in fact, as I was beginning to breakfast.

"See here," he said, "I am sent for in the Throckham case. Have you seen the report?"

As a leader writer, I had little business with the news side of my paper, and indeed I had no more than a vague recollection of some such heading as: "Tragedy in a barn," in one evening paper of the day before, and "Murder at Throckham" in another. So I could claim no very exact knowledge of the affair.

"Here you have a paper, I see," Hewitt said, reaching for it. "Perhaps their report is fuller than that in mine." He gave me his own newspaper and began searching in the other. "No," he said presently, "much the same. News agency report to both papers, no doubt."

The report which I read ran as follows:—

"SINGULAR TRAGEDY.—An extraordinary occurrence is reported from Throckham, a small village within fifteen miles of London, involving a tragic fatality that has led to a charge of murder. On Thursday evening an old barn, for some time disused, was discovered to be on fire, and it was only by extraordinary exertions on the part of the villagers that the fire was extinguished. Upon an examination of the place yesterday morning the body of Mr. Victor Peytral, a gentleman who had lived in the neighbourhood for some time, and who had been missing since shortly before the discovery of the fire, was found in the ruins. The body was burnt almost beyond recognition, but not so much as to conceal the fact that the unfortunate gentleman had not perished in the fire, but had been the victim of foul play. The throat was very deeply cut, and there can be no doubt that the murderer must have fired the barn with the object of destroying all traces of the crime. The police have arrested Mr. Percy Bowmore, a frequent visitor at the house of the deceased."

"My telegram," said Hewitt, "is plainly from a relative of this Mr. Peytral who is dead—perhaps a daughter, since she speaks of being unable to leave her mother. In that case, probably an only child, since there is no other to leave."

"Unless the others are too young," I suggested.

"Just so," Hewitt replied. "Well, Brett," he added, "to-day is Saturday."

Saturday was, of course, my "off" day, and I understood Hewitt to hint that if I pleased I might accompany him to Throckham. "Saturday it is," I said, "and I have no engagements. Would you care for me to come?"

"As you please, of course. I can guess very little of the case as yet, naturally, beyond what I have read in the paper; but the subtle sense of my experience tells me that there is all the chance of an interesting case in this. That's *your* temptation. As for myself, I don't mind admitting that—especially in these country cases, where the resources of civilisation are not always close at hand—I'm never loth to have a friend with me who isn't too proud to be made use of. That's *my* temptation!"

No persuasion was needed, and in due time we set out together.

II

It is my experience that places are to be found within twenty miles of London far more rural, far sleepier, far less influenced by the great city that lies so near, than places thrice and four times as far away. They are just too far out to be disturbed by suburban traffic, and too near to feel the influence of the great railway lines. These main lines go by, carrying their goods and their passengers to places far beyond, and it is only by awkward little branch lines, with slow and rare trains, that any part of this mid-lying belt is reached, and even then it is odds but that one must drive a good way to his destination.

Throckham was just such a place as I speak of, and that was the reason why we had such ample time to catch the first of the half-dozen leisurely trains by which one might reach the neighbourhood during the day. The station was Redfield, and Throckham was three miles beyond it.

At Redfield a coachman with a dogcart awaited Hewitt—only one gentleman having been expected, as the man explained, in offering to give either of us the reins. But Hewitt wished to talk to the coachman, and I willingly took the back seat, understanding very well that my friend would get better to work if he first had as many of the facts as possible from a calm informant before discussing them with the dead man's relations, probably confused and distracted with their natural emotions.

The coachman was a civil and intelligent fellow, and he gave Hewitt all he knew of the case with perfect clearness, as I could very well hear.

"It isn't much I can tell you, sir," he said, "beyond what I expect you know. I suppose you didn't know Mr. Peytral, my master, that's dead?"

"No. But he was a foreigner, I suppose—French, from the name."

"Well, no, sir," the coachman replied, thoughtfully; "not French exactly, I think, though sometimes he talked French to the mistress. They came from somewhere in the West Indies, I believe, and there's a trifle of—well, of dark blood in 'em, sir, I should think; though, of course, it ain't for me to say."

"Yes—there are many such families in the French West Indies. Did you ever hear of Alexandre Dumas?"

"No, sir, can't say I did."

"Well, he was a very great Frenchman indeed, but he had as much 'dark blood' as your master had—probably more; and it came from the West Indies, too. But go on."

"Mr. Peytral, you must understand, sir, has lived here a year or two—I've only been with him nine months. He talked English always—as good as you or me; and he was always called *Mr.* Peytral—not Monsieur, or Signor, or any o' them foreign titles. I think he was naturalised. Mrs. Peytral, she's an invalid—came here an invalid, I'm told. She never comes out of her bedroom 'cept on an invalid couch, which is carried. Miss Claire, she's the daughter, an' the only one, and she was hoping you'd ha' been down last night, sir, by the last train. She's in an awful state, as you may expect, sir."

"Naturally, to lose her father in such a terrible way."

"Yes, sir, but it's wuss than that even, for her. You see, this Mr. Bowmore, that they've took up, he's been sort of keepin' company with Miss Claire for some time, an' there's no doubt she was very fond of him. That makes it pretty bad for her, takin' it both ways, you see."

"Of course—terrible. But tell me how the thing happened, and why they took this Mr. Bowmore."

"Well, sir, it ain't exactly for me to say, and, of course, I don't know the rights of it, bein' only a servant, but they say there was a sudden quarrel last night between Mr. Peytral and Mr. Bowmore. I think myself that Mr. Peytral was getting a bit excitable lately, whatever it was. On Thursday night, just after dinner, he went strolling off in the dusk, alone, and presently Mr. Bowmore—he came down in the afternoon—went strolling off after him. It seems they went down toward the Penn's Meadow barn, Mr. Peytral first, and Mr. Bowmore catching him up from behind. A man saw them—a gamekeeper. He was lyin' quiet in a little wood just the other side of Penn's Meadow, an' they didn't see him as they came along together. They were quarrelling, it seems, though Grant—that's the gamekeeper— couldn't hear exactly what about; but he heard Mr. Peytral tell Mr. Bowmore to go away. He 'preferred to be alone' and he'd 'had enough' of Mr. Bowmore, from what Grant could make out. 'Get out o' my sight, sir, I tell you!' the old gentleman said at last, stamping his foot, and shaking his fist in the young gentleman's face. And then Bowmore turned and walked away."

"One moment," Hewitt interposed. "You are telling me what Grant saw and heard. How did it come to your knowledge?"

"Told me hisself, sir—told me every word yesterday. Told me twice, in fact. First thing in the morning when they found the body, and then again after he'd been to Redfield and had it took down by the police. It was because of that they arrested Mr. Bowmore, of course."

"Just so. And is this gamekeeper Grant in the same employ as yourself?"

"Oh, no, sir! Mr. Peytral's is only just an acre or two of garden and a paddock. Grant's master is Colonel White, up at the Hall."

"Very good. You were saying that Mr. Peytral told Mr. Bowmore to get out of his sight, and that Mr. Bowmore walked away. What then?"

"Well, Grant saw Mr. Bowmore walk away, but it was only a feint— a dodge, you see, sir. He walked away to the corner of the little wood where Grant was, and then he took a turn into the wood and began following Mr. Peytral up, watching him from among the trees. Came close by where Grant was sitting, following up Mr. Peytral and watching him; and so Grant lost sight of 'em."

"Did Grant say what he was doing in the wood?"

"He said he'd found marks of rabbit-snares there, and he was watching to see if anybody came to set any more."

"Yes—quite an ordinary part of his duty, of course. What next?"

"Well, Grant didn't see any more. He waited a bit, and then moved off to another part of the wood, and he didn't notice anything else particular till the barn was on fire. It was dark, then, of course."

"Yes—you must tell me about the fire. Who discovered it?"

"Oh, a man going home along the lane. He ran and called some people, and they fetched the fire-engine from the village and pumped out of the horse-pond just close by. It was pretty much of a wreck by the time they got the fire out, but it wasn't all gone, as you might have expected. You see, it had been out of use for some time, sir, and there was mostly nothing but old broken ploughs and lumber there; and what's more, there was a deal of rain early in the week, as you may remember, sir, so the thatch was pretty sodden, being out o' repair and all—and so was the timber, for the matter o' that, for there's no telling when it was last painted. So the fire didn't go quite so fierce as it might, you see; else I should expect it had been all over before they got to work on it."

"Not at all a likely sort of place to catch fire, it would seem, either," Hewitt commented. "Old ploughs and such lumber are not very combustible."

"Quite so, sir; that's what makes 'em think it so odd, I suppose. But there *was* a bundle or two of old pea-straw there, shied in last summer, they say, being over bundles from the last load, and there left."

"And when was Mr. Bowmore seen next?"

"He came strolling back, sir, and told the young lady he'd left her father outside, or something of that sort, I think; said nothing of the quarrel, I believe. But he said the barn was on fire—which he must have known pretty early, sir, for 'tis a mile from the house off that way;" and the coachman pointed with his whip.

"Nothing was suspected of the murder, it seems, till yesterday morning?"

"No, sir. Miss Claire got frightful worried when her father didn't come home, as you would expect, and specially at him not coming home all night. But when the fire was quite put out, o' course the people went away home to bed, and it wasn't till the morning that anybody went in to turn the place over. Then they found the body."

"Badly burnt, I believe?"

"Horrid burnt, sir. If it wasn't for Mr. Peytral's being missing, I doubt if they'd have known it was him at all. It took a doctor's examination to see clear that the throat had been cut. But cut it had been, and deep, so the doctor said. And now the body's gone over to Redfield mortuary."

Hewitt asked a few questions more, and got equally direct answers, except where the coachman had to confess ignorance. But presently we were at the house to which Hewitt had been summoned.

It was a pleasant house enough, standing alone, apart from the village, a little way back from a loop of road that skirted a patch of open green. As we came in at the front gate, I caught an instant's glimpse of a pale face at an upper window, and before we could reach the drawing-room door Miss Claire Peytral had met us.

She was a young lady of singular beauty, which the plain signs of violent grief and anxiety very little obscured. Her complexion, of a very delicate ivory tinge, was scarcely marred by the traces of sleeplessness and tears that were nevertheless clear to see. Her eyes were large and black, and her jetty hair had a slight waviness that was the only distinct sign about her of the remote blend of blood from an inferior race.

"Oh, Mr. Hewitt," she cried, "I am so glad you have come at last! I have been waiting—waiting so long! And my poor mother is beginning to suspect!"

"You have not told her, then?"

"No, it will kill her when she knows, I'm sure—kill her on the spot. I have only said that father is ill at—at Redfield. Oh, what shall I do?"

The poor girl seemed on the point of breakdown, and Hewitt spoke sharply and distinctly.

"What you must do is this," he said. "You must attend to me, and tell me all I want to know as accurately and as tersely as you can. In that case I will do whatever I can, but if you give way you will cripple me. It all depends on you, remember. This is my intimate friend, Mr. Brett, who is good enough to offer to help us. Now, first, I think I know the heads of the case, from the newspapers, and, more especially, from your coachman. But when you sent for me, no doubt you had some definite idea or intention in your mind. What was it?"

"Oh, he is innocent, Mr. Hewitt—he is, really! The only friend I have in the world—the only friend we all have!"

"Steady—steady," Hewitt said, pressing her kindly and firmly into a seat. "You *must* keep steady, you know, if I am to do anything. I expected that would be your belief. Now tell me why you are so sure."

"Mr. Hewitt, if you knew him you wouldn't ask. He would never injure my poor father—he went out after him purely out of kindness, because I was uneasy. He would never hurt him, Mr. Hewitt, never, never! I can't say it strongly enough—he never would! Oh! my poor father, and now — —"

"Steady again!" cried Hewitt, more sharply still. I could see that he feared the hysterical breakdown that might come at any moment after the lengthened suspense Miss Peytral had suffered. "Listen, now—you mustn't frighten yourself too much. If Mr. Bowmore is innocent—and you say you are so certain of it—then I've no doubt of finding a way to prove it if only you'll make your best effort to help me, and keep your wits about you. As far as I can see at present there's nothing against him that we need be afraid of if we tackle it properly, and, of course, the police make arrests of this sort by way of precaution in a case like this, on the merest hint. Come now, you say you were uneasy when your father went out after dinner on Thursday night. Why?"

"I don't know, quite, Mr. Hewitt. It was my mother that was uneasy, really, about something she never explained to me. My father had taken to going out in the evening after dinner, just in the way he did on Thursday night. I don't know why, but I think it had something to do with my mother's anxiety."

"Did he dress for dinner?"

"No, not lately. He used to dress always, but he has dropped it of late."

Hewitt paused for a moment, thoughtfully. Then he said, "Mrs. Peytral is an invalid, I know, and no doubt none the better for her anxiety. But if it could be managed I should like to ask her a few questions. What do you think?"

But this Miss Peytral was altogether against. Her mother was suffering from spinal complaint, it appeared, with very serious nervous complications, and there was no answering for the result of the smallest excitement. She never saw strangers, and, if it could possibly be avoided, it must be avoided now.

"Very well, Miss Peytral, I will first go and look at some things I must see, and I will do without your mother's help as long as I possibly can. But now you must answer a few more questions yourself, please."

Hewitt's questions produced little more substantial information, it seemed to me, than he had already received. Mr. Peytral had taken the house in which we were sitting—it was called "The Lodge" simply—two years ago. Before that the family had lived in Surrey, but they had not moved direct from there; there was a journey to America between, on some business of Mr. Peytral's, and it was on the return voyage that they had met Mr. Percy Bowmore. Mr. Bowmore had no friends nearer than Canada, and he was reading for the Bar—in a very desultory way, as I gathered. Miss Peytral's childhood had been passed in the West Indies, at the town of San Domingo, in fact, where her father had been a merchant. Her mother had been a helpless invalid ever since Miss Peytral could remember. As to the engagement with Bowmore, it would seem to have had the full approval of both parents all along. But a rather curious change had come over her father, she thought, a few months ago. What it was that had caused it she could not say, but he grew nervous and moody, often absent-minded, and sometimes even short-tempered and snappish, a thing she had never known before. Also he read the daily papers with much care and eagerness. It was plain that Miss Peytral had no idea of any cause which might have led to a quarrel between Bowmore and her father, and Hewitt's most cunning questions failed to elicit the smallest suggestion of reason for such an occurrence.

Ten days or so ago, Mr. Peytral had returned from a short walk after dinner, very much agitated; and from that day he had made a practice of going out immediately after dinner every evening regularly, walking off across the paddock, and so away in the direction of Penn's Meadow. The first visit of Percy Bowmore after this practice had begun was on Thursday, but the presence of the visitor made no difference, as Miss Peytral had expected it would. Her father rose abruptly after dinner and went off as before; and this time Mrs. Peytral, who had been brought down to dinner, displayed a singular uneasiness about him. She had experienced the same feeling, curiously enough, on other occasions, Miss Peytral remarked, when her husband had been unwell or in difficulties, even at some considerable distance. This time the feeling was so strong that she begged Bowmore to hurry after Mr. Peytral and accompany him in his walk. This the young man had done; but he returned alone after a while, saying simply that he had lost sight of Mr. Peytral, whom he had supposed might have come home by some other way; and mentioning also that he had been told that Penn's Meadow barn was on fire.

When it grew late, and Mr. Peytral failed to return, Bowmore went out again and made inquiry in all directions. It grew necessary to concoct a story to appease Mrs. Peytral, who had been taken back to her bedroom. Bowmore spent the whole night in fruitless search and inquiry, and then, with the morning, came the terrible news of the discovery in the burnt barn; and late in the afternoon Bowmore was arrested.

The poor girl had a great struggle to restrain her feelings during the conversation, and, at its close, Hewitt had to use all his tact to keep her going. Physical exhaustion, as well as mental trouble, were against her, and stimulus was needed. So Hewitt said, "Now you must try your best, and if you will keep up as well as you have done a little longer, perhaps I may have good news for you soon. I must go at once and examine things. First, I should like to have brought to me every single pair of boots or shoes belonging to your father. Send them, and then go and look after your mother. Remember, you are helping all the time."

III

Hewitt examined the boots and shoes with great rapidity, but with a singularly quick eye for peculiarities.

"He liked a light shoe," he said, "and he preferred to wear shoes rather than boots. There are few boots, and those not much worn, although he was living in the country. Trod square on the right foot, inward on the left, and wore the left heel more than the right. It's plain he hated nails, for these are all hand-sewn, with scarcely as much as a peg visible in the lot; and they are all laced, boots and shoes alike. Come, this is the best-worn pair; it is also a pair of the same sort the maid tells me he must have been wearing, since they are missing; low shoes, laced; we'll take them with us."

We left the house and sought our friend the coachman. He pointed out quite clearly the path by which his master had gone on his last walk; showed us the gate, still fastened, over which he had climbed to gain the adjoining meadow, and put us in the way of finding the small wood and the barn.

Both within and without the gate there was a small patch bare of grass, worn by feet; and here Martin Hewitt picked up his trail at once.

"The ground has hardened since Thursday night," he said; "and so much the better—it keeps the marks for us. Do you see what is here?"

There were footmarks, certainly, but so beaten and confused that I could make nothing of them. Hewitt's practised eye, however, read them as I might have read a rather illegibly written letter.

"Here is the right foot, plain enough," he said, carefully fitting the shoe he had brought in the mark. "He alighted on that as he came over the gate. Half over it is another footmark—Bowmore's, I expect, for I can see signs of others, in both directions—going and coming. But we shall know better presently."

He rose, and we followed the irregular track across the meadow. Like most such field-tracks, its direction was plainly indicated by the thin and beaten grass, with a bare spot here and there. Hewitt troubled to take no more than a glance at each of these spots as we passed, but that was all he needed. The meadow was bounded by a hedge, with a stile; and at the farther side of this stile my friend knelt again, with every sign of attention.

"A little piece of luck," he reported. "The left shoe has picked up a tiny piece of broken thorn-twig just here. See the mark? The shoe was a little soddened in the sole by this time, and the thorn stuck. I hope it stuck altogether. If it did it may help us wonderfully when we get to the barn, for the trouble there will be the trampling all round of the people at the fire."

So we went on till we reached the edge of the little wood. The field-path skirted this, and here Hewitt dropped on his knees and set to work with great minuteness.

"Keep away from the track, Brett," he warned me, "or you may make it worse. The police have been here, I see, and quite recently, coming from the direction of Redfield. Here are two pairs of unmistakable police boots and another heavy pair with them; no doubt they brought the gamekeeper along with them, to have things fully explained."

From the corner of the wood to a point forty yards along the path; back to the corner again, and then into the wood Hewitt went, carefully examining every inch of the ground as he did so. Then at last he rejoined me.

"I think the gamekeeper has told the truth," he said. "It's pretty plain, thanks to the soft ground hereabout, notwithstanding the policemen's boots. Here they came together—the thorn-twig sticks to the shoe still, you see—and here they stopped. The marks face about, and Bowmore's steps are retraced to the corner of the wood. Peytral's turn again and go on, and Bowmore's turn into the edge of the wood and come along among the trees. You don't see them in the grassy parts quite as well as I do, I expect, but there they are. We'll keep after Peytral's prints. Bowmore's come back in the same track, I see."

The next stile led to Penn's Meadow. This meadow—a large one—stretched over a rather steep hump of land, at the other side of which the barn stood. From the stile two paths could be discerned—one rising straight over the meadow in the direction of the barn, and the other skirting it to the left, parallel with the hedge.

"Here the footprints part," Hewitt observed, musingly; "and what does that mean? Man[oe]uvring—or what?"

He thought a moment, and then went on: "We'll leave the tracks for the present and see the barn. That is straight ahead, I take it."

When we reached the top of the rise the barn came in view, a blackened and sinister wreck. The greater part of the main structure was still standing, and even part of the thatched roof still held its place, scorched and broken. Off to the right from where we stood the village roofs were visible, giving indication of the position of the road to Redfield. A single human figure was in sight—that of a policeman on guard before the barn.

"Now we must get rid of that excellent fellow," said Hewitt, "or he'll be offering objections to the examination I want to make. I wonder if he knows my name?"

We walked down to the barn, and Hewitt, assuming the largest possible air, addressed the policeman.

"Constable," he said, "I am here officially—here is my card. Of course you will know the name if you have had any wide experience—London experience especially. I am looking into this case on behalf of Miss Peytral—co-operating with the police, of course. Where is your inspector?"

He was a rather stupid countryman, this policeman, but he was visibly impressed—even flurried—by Hewitt's elaborate bumptiousness. He saluted, tried to look unnaturally sagacious, and confessed that he couldn't exactly say where the inspector was, things being put about so just now. He might be in Throckham village, but more likely he was at Redfield.

"Ah!" Hewitt replied, with condescension. "Now, if he is in the village, you will oblige me, constable, by telling him that I am here. If he is not there, you will return at once. I will be responsible here till you come back. Don't be very long, now."

The man was taken by surprise, and possibly a trifle doubtful. But Hewitt was so extremely lofty and so very peremptory and official, that the inferior intelligence capitulated feebly, and presently, after another uneasy salute, the village policeman had vanished in the direction of the road. The moment he had disappeared Hewitt turned to the ruined barn. The door was gone, and the scorched and charred lumber that littered the place had a look of absolute ghostliness—perhaps chiefly the effect of my imagination in the knowledge of the ghastly tragedy that the place had witnessed. Well in from the doorway was a great scatter of light ashes—plainly the pea-straw that the coachman had spoken of. And by these ashes and partly among them, marked in some odd manner on the floor, was a horrible black shape that I shuddered to see, as Hewitt pointed it out with a moving forefinger, which he made to trace the figure of a prostrate human form.

"Did you never see that before in a burnt house?" Hewitt asked in a hushed voice. "I have, more than once. That sort of thing always leaves a strange stain under it, like a shadow."

But business claimed Martin Hewitt, and he stepped carefully within. Scarcely had he done so, when he stood suddenly still, with a low whistle, pointing toward something lying among the dirt and ashes by the foot of that terrible shape.

"See?" he said. "Don't disturb anything, but look!"

I crept in with all the care I could command, and stooped. The place was filled with such a vast confusion of lumber and cinder and ash that at first I failed to see at all what had so startled Hewitt's attention. And even when I understood his direction, all I saw was about a dozen little wire loops, each a quarter of an inch long or less, lying among a little grey ash that clung about the ends of some of the loops in clots. Even as I looked another thing caught Hewitt's eye. Among the straw-ashes there lay some cinders of paper and card, and near them another cinder, smaller, and plainly of some other substance. Hewitt took my walking-stick, and turned this cinder over. It broke apart as he did so, and from within it two or three little charred sticks escaped. Hewitt snatched one up and scrutinised it closely.

"Do you see the tin ferrule?" he said. "It has been a brush; and that was a box of colours!" He pointed to the cinder at his feet. "That being so," he went on, "that paper and card was probably a sketch-book. Brett! come outside a bit. There's something amazing here!"

We went outside, and Hewitt faced me with a curious expression that for the life of me I could not understand.

"Suppose," he said, "*that Mr. Victor Peytral is not dead after all?*"

"Not dead?" I gasped; "but—but he is! We know——"

"It seems to me," Hewitt pursued, with his eyes still fixed on mine, "that we know very little indeed of this affair, as yet. The body was unrecognisable, or very near it. You remember what the coachman said? 'If it wasn't for Mr. Peytral's being missing,' he said, 'I doubt if they'd have known it was him at all.' I think those were his exact words. More, you must remember that the body has not been seen by either of Peytral's relatives."

"But then," I protested, "if it isn't his body whose is it?"

"Ah, indeed," Hewitt responded, "whose is it? Don't you see the possibilities of the thing? There's a colour-box and a sketch-book burned. Who carried a colour-box and a sketch-book? Not Peytral, or we should have heard of it from his daughter; she made a particular point of her father's evening strolls being quite aimless, so far as her knowledge or conjecture went; she knew nothing of any sketching. And another thing—don't you see what *those* things mean?" He pointed toward the place of the little wire loops.

"Not at all."

"Man, don't you see they've been boot-buttons? When the boots shrivelled, the threads were burnt and the buttons dropped off. Boot-buttons are made of a sort of composition that burns to a grey ash, once the fire really gets hold of them—as you may try yourself, any time you please. You can see the ash still clinging to some of the shanks; and there the shanks are, lying in two groups, six and six, as they fell! Now Peytral came out in laced shoes."

"But if Peytral isn't dead, where is he?"

"Precisely," rejoined Hewitt, with the curious expression still in his eyes. "As you say, where is he? And as you said before, who is the dead man? Who is the dead man, and where is Peytral, and why has he gone? Don't you see the possibilities of the case *now*?"

Light broke upon me suddenly. I saw what Hewitt meant. Here was a possible explanation of the whole thing—Peytral's recent change of temper, his evening prowlings, his driving away of Bowmore, and lastly, of his disappearance—his flight, as it now seemed probable it was. The case had taken a strange turn, and we looked at one another with meaning eyes. It might be that Hewitt, begged by the unhappy girl we had but just left to prove the innocence of her lover, would by that very act bring her father to the gallows.

"Poor girl!" Hewitt murmured, as we stood staring at one another. "Better she continued to believe him dead, as she does! Brett, there's many a good man would be disposed to fling these proofs away for the girl's sake and her mother's, seeing how little there can be to hurt Bowmore. But justice must be done, though the blow fall—as it commonly does—on innocent and guilty together. See, now, I've another idea. Stay on guard while I try."

He hurried out toward the farther side of the broad band of trampled ground which surrounded the burnt barn, and began questing to and fro, this way and that, receding farther from me as he went, and nearing the horse-pond and the road. At last he vanished altogether, and left me alone with the burnt barn, my thoughts, and—that dim Shape on the barn floor. It was broad day, but I felt none too happy; and I should not have been at all anxious to keep the police watch at night.

Perhaps Hewitt had been gone a quarter of an hour, perhaps a little more, when I saw him again, hurrying back and beckoning to me. I went to meet him.

"It's right enough," he cried. "I've come on his trail again! There it is, thorn-mark and all, by the roadside, and at a stile—going to Redfield—probably to the station. Come, we'll follow it up! Where's that fool of a policeman? Oh, the muddle they *can* make when they really try!"

"Need we wait for him?" I asked.

"Yes, better now, with those proofs lying there; and we must tell him not to be bounced off again as I bounced him off. There he comes!"

The heavy figure of the local policeman was visible in the distance, and we shouted and beckoned to hurry him. Agility was no part of that policeman's nature, however, and beyond a sudden agitation of his head and his shoulders, which we guessed to be caused by a dignified spasm of leisurely haste, we saw no apparent acceleration of his pace.

As we stood and waited we were aware of a sound of wheels from the direction of Redfield, and as the policeman neared us from the right, so the sound of wheels approached us from the left. Presently a fly hove in sight—the sort of dusty vehicle that plies at every rural railway station in this country; and as he caught sight of us in the road the driver began waving his whip in a very singular and excited manner. As he drew nearer still he shouted, though at first we could not distinguish his words. By this time the policeman, trotting ponderously, was within a few yards. The passenger in the fly, a thin, dark, elderly man, leaned over the side to look ahead at us, and with that the policeman pulled up with a great gasp and staggered into the ditch.

"'Ere 'e is!" cried the fly-driver, regardless of the angry remonstrances of his fare. "'Ere 'e is! 'E's all right! It ain't 'im! 'Ere he is!"

"Shut your mouth, you fool!" cried the angry fare. "*Will* you stop making a show of me?"

"Not me!" cried the eccentric cabman. "I don't want no fare, sir! I'm drivin' you 'ome for honour an' glory, an' honour an' glory I'll make it! 'Ere 'e is!"

Hewitt took in the case in a flash—the flabbergasted policeman, the excited cabman and the angry passenger. He sprang into the road and cried to the cabman, who pulled up suddenly before us.

"Mr. Victor Peytral, I believe?" said Martin Hewitt.

"Yes, sir," answered the dark gentleman snappishly, "but I don't know you!"

"There has been a deal of trouble here, Mr. Peytral, over your absence from home, as no doubt you have become aware; and I was telegraphed for by your daughter. My name is Hewitt—Martin Hewitt."

Peytral's face changed instantly. "I know your name well, Mr. Hewitt," he said. "There's a matter—but who is this?"

"My friend, Mr. Brett, who is good enough to help me to-day. If I may detain you a moment, I should like a word with you aside."

"Certainly."

Mr. Peytral alighted, and the two walked a little apart.

I saw Hewitt talking and pointing toward the burnt barn, and I well guessed what he was saying. He was giving Peytral warning of what he had discovered in the barn, explaining that he must give the information to the police, and asking if, in those circumstances, Peytral wished to go home, or to make other arrangements. Often Hewitt's duty to his clients and his duty as a law-upholding citizen between them put him in some such delicate position.

But there was no hesitation in Mr. Victor Peytral. Plainly he feared nothing, and he was going home.

"Very well, then," I heard Hewitt say as they turned towards us, "perhaps we had better go on slowly and let my friend cut across the fields first to break the news. Brett—I knew you would be useful, sooner or later."

And so I hurried off, with the happy though delicate mission to restore both father and lover to Miss Claire Peytral.

IV

Miss Peytral had to be put to bed under care of a nurse, for the revulsion was very great, and so was her physical prostration. Bowmore, now set free, and in himself a very pleasant young fellow, came with hurried inquiries and congratulations, and then rushed off to London to cable to his friends in Canada, for fear of the effect of newspaper telegrams.

When at last Hewitt and I sat with Mr. Peytral in his study, "Mr. Hewitt," said Peytral, "I am not sure how far explanations may go between us. There is more in that death in the barn than the police will ever guess."

Peytral was haggard and drawn, for, as he had let slip already, he had scarce slept an hour since leaving home on Thursday.

"I am tired," he said, "and worn out, but that is not a novelty with me; and I'm not sure but we may be of use to each other. Did my daughter tell you why she sent Mr. Bowmore after me on Thursday night?"

Hewitt explained the thing as briefly as possible, just as he had heard it from Miss Peytral.

"Ah," said Peytral, thoughtfully. "So she thought my manner became moody a few months back. It did, no doubt, for I had memories; and more, I had apprehensions. Mr. Hewitt, I think I read in the papers that you were in some way engaged in the extraordinary case of the murder of Mr. Jacob Mason?"

"That is quite correct. I was."

"There was another case, a little while before, which possibly you may not have heard of. A man was found strangled near the York column, by Pall Mall, with just such a mark on his forehead as was found on Mr. Mason's."

"I know that case, too, as well as the other."

"Do you know the name of the murderer?"

"I think I do. We speak in confidence, of course, as client and professional man?"

"Of course. What was his name?"

"I have heard two—Everard Myatt and Catherton Hunt."

"Neither is his real name, and I doubt if anybody but himself knows it. Twenty years ago and more I knew him as Mayes. He was a Jamaican. Mr. Hewitt, that man's foul life has been justly forfeit a thousand times, but if it belongs to anybody it belongs to me!"

It was terrible to see the sudden fiery change in the old man. His lassitude was gone in a flash, his eyes blazed and his nostrils dilated.

For a little while he sat so, his mouth awork with passion; then he sank back in his chair with a sigh.

"I am getting old," he said, more quietly, "and perhaps I am not strong enough to lose my temper.... Well, as I said, Mayes was a Jamaican, a renegade white. Do you remember that in the black rebellion of 1865, there was a traitorous white man among the negroes? Eyre hanged a few rebels, and rightly, but the worst creature on all that island escaped—probably escaped by the aid of that very white skin that should have ensured him a greater punishment than the rest. He escaped to Hayti. Now you have probably heard something of Hayti, and of the common state of affairs there?"

We both had heard, and, indeed, the matter had been particularly brought to Hewitt's notice by the case which I have told elsewhere as "The Affair of the Tortoise." As for me, I had read Sir Spenser St. John's book on the black republic, and I had been greatly impressed by the graphic picture it gives of the horrible, blood-stained travesty of regular government there prevailing. Nothing in the worst of the South American Republics is to be remotely compared to it. In the worst periods there was not a crime imaginable that could not be, and was not, committed openly and with impunity by anybody on the right side of the so-called "government"; and the "government" was nothing but an organised crime in itself.

"Well," Peytral pursued, "then I need not expatiate on it, and you will understand the sort of place that Mayes fled to, and how it suited him. He was a man of far greater ability than any of the coarse scoundrels in power, and he was worse than all of them. He was not such a fool as to aim at ostensible political power—that way generally led to assassination. He was the jackal, the contriver, the power behind the throne, the instigator of half the devilry set going in that unhappy place, and he profited by it with little risk; he was the confidential adviser of that horrible creature Domingue. If you know anything of Hayti you will know what that means.

"At this time I was comparatively a young man, and a merchant at Port-au-Prince. It was a bad place, of course, and business was risky enough, but, for that very reason, profits were large, and that was an attraction to a sanguine young man like myself. I did very well, and I had thoughts of getting out of it with what I had made. But it was a fatal thing to be supposed wealthy in Port-au-Prince, unless you were a villain in power, or partner with one. I was neither, and I was judged a suitable victim by Mayes. Not I alone, either—no, nor even only I and my fortune. Gentlemen, gentlemen, my poor wife, who now lies— —"

Peytral's utterance failed him. He rose as if choking, and Hewitt rose to quiet him. "Never mind," he said, "sit quiet now. We understand. Rest a moment."

The old man sank back in his chair, and for a little while buried his face in his hands. Then he went on.

"I needn't go into details," he said, huskily. "It is enough to say that every devilish engine of force and cunning was put in operation against me. So it came that at last, on a hint from a hanger-on of the police-office, who had enough humanity in him to remember a kindness he had experienced at my hands, that we took flight in the middle of the night—my poor wife, myself, and our three children, with nothing in the world but our bare lives and the clothes we wore. I might have tried to get aboard a foreign ship in the harbour, but I knew that would be useless. I should have been given up on whatever criminal charge Mayes chose to present, and my wife and children with me. I had hope of somehow getting to San Cristobel, where I had a friend—over the border in the other Government of the island, the Dominican Republic. That was eighty miles away and more, across swamps, and forests and mountains. Well, we did it— we did it. We did it, Mr. Hewitt, and I dream of it still. They hunted us, sir—hunted us with dogs. We hid from them a whole day among the rank weeds—up to our shoulders in the water of a pestilential fever-swamp; Claire, the baby, on her mother's back, and both the boys on mine. They died—they died next day. My two beautiful boys, gentlemen, died in my arms, and I was too weak even to bury them!"

There was another long pause, and the man's head was bowed in his hands once more. Presently he went on again, but at first without lifting his head.

"We did it, gentlemen," he said—"we did it. We crawled into San Cristobel at the end of five days; and from that moment my dear wife has never once stood upright on her feet. So we came out of it, and the baby, Claire, was the one that suffered least. She was too young to understand, and her mother—her mother saved her, when I could not save the boys!"

He paused again, and presently sat up, pale, but in full command of himself. "You will excuse me, gentlemen, I am sure, and make allowances for my feelings," he said. "There is not a great deal more to tell. Mayes did not last long in Hayti. Domingue was overthrown, and Mayes left the island, I was told, and made for another part of the world. Years afterward I heard of his being in China, though what truth there may have been in the rumour I cannot say.

"My friend in San Cristobel—he was a cousin, in fact—put me on my legs again, and after a while he helped me to begin business at San Domingo, under my present name, Peytral, which, in fact, was my mother's maiden name. There came a sudden push in trade with the United States about this time, and I went into my affairs with the more energy to distract my thoughts. In fifteen years—to cut a long story short—I had made the small competency which I have brought to England with me, with the idea of a peaceful end to my life and my wife's; though I doubt if I am to have that now. I doubt it, and I will tell you why. Mr. Hewitt, when I went away without warning on Thursday night I was dogging Mayes!"

Hewitt nodded, with no sign of surprise. "And the man killed in the barn?"

"That is one more of his thousand crimes, without a doubt. Though it differs. Do you know what drew my attention to the murders of the men Denson and Mason, and so set me thinking? In each case the murder was by strangulation, and the medical evidence at the inquests showed that it was effected by means of a tourniquet. In fact, in the second case, the tourniquet itself was left behind."

"Yes," Hewitt replied, "I loosened it myself—but, unfortunately, I was too late."

"Well, now," Peytral went on, "in Hayti, in my time, Mayes's enemies had a habit of dying suddenly in the night, by strangulation, and a tourniquet was always the instrument. And just as murder was quite a popular procedure in that accursed place, so strangulation by tourniquet became for a while the most common form of the crime. It was rapid, effective, and silent, you see. So that a murder by tourniquet, quite an unknown thing in this country, took my attention at once, and when another followed it so soon, I felt something like certainty. And the triangle was suggestive, too."

"Were Mayes's victims marked in that way in Hayti?"

"No, there was no mark. But"—here Mr. Peytral's features assumed a curious expression—"there are things which are not believed in this country—which are laughed at, in fact, and called superstition. You know something of Hayti, and therefore you must have heard of Voodoo—the witchcraft and devil-worship of the West Indies. Well, Mayes was as deep in that as he was in every other species of wickedness. It sounds foolish, perhaps, here in civilised England, and you may laugh, but I tell you that Mayes could make men do as he wished, with their consent or against it! And he used a thing—it was generally known that he used a thing marked with a triangle—a Red Triangle—by the use of which he could bend men to his will!"

Hewitt was listening intently, with no sign of laughter at all, notwithstanding his client's apprehension. And I remembered the case of Mr. Jacob Mason, and how that victim had so fervently expressed his wish to the excellent clergyman, Mr. Potswood, that he had never dabbled in the strange devilries of Myatt—or Mayes, as we were now learning to call him.

"At any rate," Peytral resumed, "you will understand that the conjunction of the tourniquet with the Red Triangle in the two cases you know of caused me some excitement. My daughter, as you have said, noticed a change in my habits from that time; my wife did more—she knew the reason. Mr. Hewitt, I am an older man, but there is hotter blood in my veins than in yours. My father was English—though you might scarcely suppose it—but my mother, to whose name I have reverted, was a French Creole. So perhaps my natural instincts come nearer to those of our savage ancestry than do yours. Whether or not you will understand me I do not know, but I can tell you that even now, in cold blood—for my paroxysm has exhausted itself and me—it seems to me that it would be my duty, not to say my sacred duty, to tear that man to pieces with my hands whenever and wherever I could put them on him! My old passions may have slept, I find, but they are alive still, and I found them waking when I realised that Mayes was alive and in England. The words 'sane' and 'insane' are elastic in their application, but I doubt if you would have called me strictly sane of late. I evolved mad schemes for the destruction of this wretch, and I was ready to devote myself and everything I possessed to the purpose. More than once I contemplated coming to you—seeing that you had met the man in one of his villainies—with the idea of enlisting your aid. But I reflected that you would probably make yourself no party to a plan of private revenge, and I hesitated. And then—then, a little more than a week ago, I saw the man himself! Changed, without doubt, but not half as much changed as I am myself. Nevertheless, sure as I am of him now, I hesitated then. For it was here in the meadow that you know, near the barn, and the thing seemed so likely to be illusion that I almost suspected my senses. It was dusk, and he was walking and talking with another man, a good deal younger. And presently, while I was still confounded with surprise, and as they passed behind a clump of trees, Mayes was gone, and I saw his companion alone. He was a young man—an artist, it would seem, with sketch-book and colours."

I started, and Hewitt and I glanced at each other. Peytral saw it and paused. "Never mind," said Hewitt. "Please go on."

"After that I came out every night, in the hope of seeing my enemy again. On several evenings I saw the young artist waiting by the barn expectantly, but nobody joined him. I found that this young man was lodging at a cottage in the village, and I resolved not to lose sight of him.

"At last, on Thursday night, I saw Mayes again. Mr. Bowmore was here, and when I left the house he troubled me much by coming after me. I was obliged to tell him that I wished to be alone, and I was in a nervously explosive state when I did it. He seemed reluctant to go; my anger blazed out, and I violently ordered him off. From what he has told me it seems that he followed me still, but lost sight of me near Penn's Meadow. Well, be that as it may, I saw Mayes and the young artist again. I watched from a rather awkward spot, and dusk was falling, so that I could not see all that passed; but presently I was aware that Mayes was making off by the road alone, and I followed him.

"From that moment I think I really was mad, though my madness did not drive me to attack him at once. I had a feeling of curiosity to see where he would go, and a curious cruel idea of letting him run for a little first—as a cat feels, I suppose, with a mouse. You may judge that I was not in my normal state of mind from the fact that all through yesterday and part of to-day I never as much as thought of telegraphing home to say that I had gone to London. For it was to London I followed him. I took no ticket at the station—I got on the platform by stealth, and entered the train unobserved, for he and one boy were the only passengers, and I feared attracting attention. It was easy enough, in such a station as Redfield, and I paid my fare at London. And after all I lost him! Lost him in London!"

"How?"

"Like a fool. I saw him enter a house, and waited. Followed him again, and waited at another. I might have flung him into the river from the Embankment, and I refrained. And then—whether it began at a dark corner or in a group of people I cannot tell, but I suddenly discovered that I was following a stranger—a stranger of about Mayes's form and stature. It was what I should have expected, and provided for, in London streets at night!

"If I have been mad, it was then I was worst. I suppose by that time it must have been too late to get back home, but I never thought of that. I ran the streets the whole night, like a fool, hunting for Mayes. I kept on all day yesterday. I waited and watched hours at the two houses he had visited; and it was not till early this morning that I flung myself on a bed in a private hotel in Euston Road. I slept a little, and my paroxysm was over. Perhaps I am more fortunate than I am disposed to think, since I am as yet in no danger of trial for murder."

This passionate, wayward, stricken man was plainly the object of fascinated interest to Hewitt. My friend waited a moment, and then said—"The houses he called at—I should like to know them. And where you lost sight of him."

Peytral sat back, and gazed thoughtfully for fully half a minute in Hewitt's face. "Do you know," he said at length, "I don't think I'll answer that question now. I'd like to leave it for a day or two. Yesterday I wouldn't have told you, even on the rack—no, not a word! I should have said, 'Take your own chances, and get him if you can. As for me, I consider him *my* prey, and what scent I have picked up I shall use myself!' A mad fancy, you will think, perhaps. For me the question is, was I sanest then or now? I will take a day or two to think."

V

In less than a day or two the identity of the victim of the burnt barn was established. For Hewitt had his idea, and he communicated with Plummer, of Scotland Yard. The man with the buttoned boots and the sketch-book was the artist who had been staying at the cottage in the village, but who, singularly enough, had never been seen to draw, and had left no drawings behind him. He had warned the people of the cottage that he might be away for a night or two, and he had stayed away for two nights before; so that his disappearance did not disturb them, and when they heard that Mr. Peytral's body had been found in the barn they accepted the news as fact. They recognised at once a photograph produced by Plummer as that of their late lodger. And the photograph had been procured from Messrs. Kingsley, Bell and Dalton, the intended victims in the bond case, and it was one of Henning, their vanished correspondence clerk!

That his death would be convenient to Mayes, the greater scoundrel, was plain enough. The bond robbery had been brought to naught, thanks to Martin Hewitt, and Henning was now useless. Worse, he might be caught, or give himself up, and was thus a perpetual danger. And probably he wanted money. This being so, it was a singular fact that at the inquest the surgeon who had examined the wound gave it as his most positive opinion that it had been self-inflicted. And it was inflicted with a razor, Henning's own, as was very clearly proved after inquiry. For the razor was found in the barn by the police, entangled with the blackened frame of an old lantern. Here was still another puzzle; one to which the final revelation of the mystery of the Red Triangle gave an answer, as will be seen in due place.

THE CASE OF THE ADMIRALTY CODE

I

Quick on the heels of the case of the Burnt Barn followed the next of the Red Triangle affairs. Indeed, the interval was barely two days. Mr. Victor Peytral, it will be remembered, had declined to reveal to Hewitt the addresses of the two houses in London which he had seen Mayes visit, desiring to think the matter over for a few days first; but before any more could be heard from him, news of another sort was brought by Inspector Plummer.

It may give some clue to the period whereabout the whole mystery of the Red Triangle began to be cleared up if I say that at the time of Plummer's visit this country was on the very verge of war with a great European State. It is a State with which the present relations of England are of the friendliest description, and, since the dreaded collision was happily averted, there is no need to particularise in the matter now, especially as the name of the country with which we were at variance matters nothing as regards the course of events I am to relate. Though most readers will recognise it at once when I say that the war, had it come to that, would have been a naval war of great magnitude; and that during the time of tension swift but quiet preparations were going forward at all naval depôts, and movements and dispositions of our fleet were arranged that extended to the remotest parts of the ocean.

It was at the height of the excitement, and, as I have said, two days after the return of Hewitt and myself from Throckham, when the case of the Burnt Barn had been disposed of, that Detective-Inspector Plummer called. I was in Hewitt's office at the time, having, in fact, called in on my way to learn if he had heard more from Mr. Victor Peytral, for, as may be imagined, I was as eager to penetrate the mystery of the Triangle as Hewitt himself—perhaps more so, since Hewitt was a man inured to mysteries. I had hardly had time to learn that Peytral had not yet made up his mind so far as to write, when Plummer pushed hurriedly into the room.

"Excuse my rushing in like this," he said, "but your lad told me that it was Mr. Brett who was with you, and the matter needs hurry. You've heard no more of that fellow—Myatt, Hunt, Mayes, whatever his name is last—since the barn murder, of course? Has Peytral given you the tip he half promised?"

Hewitt shook his head again. "Brett has this moment come to ask the same question," he said. "I have heard nothing."

"I must have it," said Plummer, emphatically. "Do you think he will tell me?"

Hewitt shook his head again. "Scarcely likely," he said. "He's an odd fellow, this Mr. Peytral—a foreigner, with revenge in his blood. I have done him and his daughter some little service, and he told me all his private history; but he seemed even then disposed to keep Mayes to himself and let nobody interfere with his own vengeance. But I will wire if you like. What is it?"

"I'll tell you," said Plummer, pushing the door close behind him. "I'll tell you—in confidence, of course—because you've seen more of this mysterious rascal than I have, and—equally in confidence, of course—Mr. Brett may hear, too, since he's been in several of the cases already. Well, of course, we all know well enough that we want this creature—Mayes, we may as well call him, I suppose, now—for three murders, at least, to say nothing of other things. That's all very well, and we might have got him with time. But now we want him for something else; and it's such a thing that *we must have him at once*, or else"—and Plummer pursed his lips and snapped his fingers significantly. "We can't wait over this, Mr. Hewitt; *we've got to have that man to-day*, if it can be done. And there's more than ordinary depending on it. It's the country this time. The Admiralty telegraphic code has been stolen!"

"By Mayes?"

Plummer shrugged his shoulders. "That's to be proved," he said; "but he was seen leaving the office at about the time the loss occurred, and that's enough to set me after him; and there's not another clue of any sort. Mr. Hewitt, I wish you were in the official service!"

Hewitt smiled. "You flatter me," he said, "as you have done before. But why in this case particularly?"

"It's a case altogether out of the ordinary, and one of a string of such, all of which you have at your fingers' ends. And I don't mind confessing that this man Mayes is a little too big a handful for one—for me, at any rate. I wish you could work with me over this; in fact, in the special circumstances I've a good mind to ask to have you retained, as an exceptional measure. But the thing's urgent, and there's red-tape!"

Hewitt had taken a glance at his desk tablet, which he now flung down.

"I'll do it for love," he said, "if necessary. My appointment list is uncommonly slack just now, and even if it weren't, I'd make a considerable sacrifice rather than be out of this. This fellow Mayes is a dangerous man; and I feel it a point of honour that he shall not continue to escape. Moreover, I have begun to form a certain theory as to the Red Triangle, and all there is at the back of it—a theory I would rather keep to myself till I see a little more, since as it stands it may only strike you as fantastic, and if it is wrong it may lead some of us off the track; but it is a theory I wish to test to the end. So I'm with you, Plummer, if you'll allow it; and you can make your official application for a special retainer or not, just as you please."

Plummer was plainly delighted.

"Most certainly I will," he said. "Shall I give you the heads of the case, or will you come to the Admiralty and see for yourself?"

"Both, I think," said Hewitt. "But first I will send a telegram to Peytral. Then you can give me the heads of the case as we go along, and I will look at the place for myself. I am in this case heart and soul, pay or no pay—and I expect my friend Brett would like to be in it, too. Is there any objection?"

"Well," Plummer answered, a little doubtfully, "we're glad of outside help, of course, but I'm not sure, officially——"

"Of course you are always glad of outside help," Hewitt interrupted, "and in this case we may possibly find Brett more useful than you think. Consider now. He has seen a good deal of these cases—quite as much as you, in fact—but he is the only one of the three of us whom Mayes does not know by sight. Remember, Mayes saw us both in the affair of Mr. Jacob Mason, and he saw you again in the case of the Lever Key—escaped, in fact, because he instantly recognised you. I'll answer for Brett's discretion, and I'm sure he'll be glad to help, even if, for official reasons, you may not find it possible to admit him wholly into your counsels."

Of course I willingly assented, and the conditions understood, Plummer offered no further objection. Hewitt despatched his telegram, and in a very few minutes we were in a cab on the way to the Admiralty.

"This is the way of it," Plummer said. "You will remember that when we lost Mayes at the end of the Lever Key case, I was waiting for him in that city office, with an assistant, and that we only saw him for an instant in the lift. Well, that assistant was a very intelligent man of mine, named Corder—a fellow with a wonderful memory for a face. Now Corder is on another case just now, and we'd put him on, dressed like a loafer, to hang about Whitehall and the neighbourhood, watching for some one we want. Well, this morning there came an urgent message to the Yard from the Admiralty, to ask for a responsible official at once, and I was sent. As I came along I saw Corder lounging about, and of course I took no notice—it would not do for us people from the Yard to recognise each other too readily in the street. But Corder came up, and made pretence to ask me for a match to light his pipe; and under cover of that he told me that he had seen Mayes not an hour before, coming out of the Admiralty. At this, of course, I pricked up my ears. I didn't know what they wanted me for, but if there was mischief, and that fellow had been there, it was likely at least that he might have been in it. Corder was quite positive that it was the man, although he had only seen him for a moment in the lift. He hadn't seen him go into the Admiralty office, but he was passing as he came out, and noted the time exactly, so that he might report to me at the first opportunity. The time was 11.32, and Mayes jumped into a hansom and drove off. He walked right out into the middle of the road to stop the hansom—you know how wide the road is there—so that Corder couldn't hear his direction to the cabman, but he took the number as the cab went off. Corder ought to have collared him then and there, I think, but he was in a difficult position. It would have endangered the case he was on, which is very important; and besides, he didn't realise how much we wanted him for, having only been brought in as an assistant at the tail of our bond case. Still less did he guess—any more than myself—what I was going to hear at the Admiralty office."

"At any rate," interrupted Hewitt, "you've got the number of the cab?"

"Here it is," Plummer answered, "and I've already set a man to get hold of the cabman. You'd better note the number—92,873."

Hewitt duly noted the number, and advised me to do the same, in case I should chance to meet the cab during the afternoon; and as we neared our destination Plummer gave us the rest of the case in outline.

"In the office," he said, "I found them in a great state. A copy of the code, or cypher, in which confidential orders and other messages are sent to the fleet all over the world, and in which reports and messages are sent back, had disappeared during the morning. It was in charge of a Mr. Robert Telfer, a clerk of responsibility and undoubted integrity. He kept it in a small iron safe, which is let into the wall of his private room. It was safe when he arrived in the morning, and he immediately used it in order to code a telegram, and locked it in the safe again at 10.20. Two hours later, at 12.20, he went to the safe for it again, in order to de-code a message just received, and it was gone! And the lock of the safe is one that would take hours to pick, I should judge. There isn't a shade of a clue, so far as I can see, except this circumstance of Mayes being seen leaving by Corder—just between Telfer's two visits to the safe, you perceive. And of course there may be nothing in that, except for the character of the man. And that's all there is to go on, as far as I can see. I needn't tell you how important the thing is at a time like this, and how much would be paid for that secret code by a certain foreign Government. We have made hurried arrangements to have certain places watched, and as soon as I have taken you to the office I must rush off and make a few more arrangements still. But here we are."

Mr. Robert Telfer's room was at the side of a long and gloomy corridor on the upper floor, and the door was distinguished merely by a number and the word "Private" painted thereon. We found Mr. Telfer sitting alone, and plainly in a state of great nervous tension. He was a man of forty or thereabout, thin, alert, and using a single eye-glass. Plummer introduced us by name, and rapidly explained our business.

"I told you the name of the party I am after, Mr. Telfer," Plummer said, "and I went straight to Mr. Martin Hewitt, as being most likely to have information of him. Mr. Hewitt, whose name you know already, of course, is kind enough, seeing we're in a bad pinch, and pushed for time, to come in and give us all the help he can. Both he and his friend, Mr. Brett, know a good deal of the doings of the person we're after, and their assistance is likely to be of the very greatest value. Do you mind giving Mr. Hewitt any information he may ask? I must rush over to the Yard to put some other inquiries on foot, and to set an observation or two, but I'll be back presently."

"Certainly," Mr. Telfer answered, "I'm only too anxious to give any information whatever—so long as it is nothing departmentally forbidden—which will help to put this horrible matter right. Please ask me anything, and be patient if my answers are not very clear. I have been much overworked lately, as you may imagine, and have had very little sleep; and now this terrible misfortune has upset me completely; for, of course, I am held responsible for that copy of the code, and if it isn't recovered, and quickly, I am ruined—to say nothing, of course, of the far more serious consequences in other directions."

"That is the safe in which it was kept, I presume?" Hewitt said, indicating a small one let into the wall. "May I examine it?"

"Certainly." Mr. Telfer turned and produced the keys from his pocket. "The code was here, lying on this shelf when I needed it this morning at ten. I took it out, used it, returned it to the same place exactly, and locked the safe door. Then I took the draft of the telegram, together with the copy in cypher, into the Controller's room, gave it into safe hands, and returned here."

Hewitt narrowly examined the lock of the safe with his pocket lens. "There are no signs of the lock having been picked," he said, "even if that were possible. As a matter of fact, this is a lock that would take half a day to pick, even with a heavy bag of tools. No, I don't think that was the way of it. You have no doubt about locking the safe door at 10.20, I suppose, before you went to the Controller's room?"

"No possible doubt whatever. You see, I left the whole bunch of keys hanging in the lock while I coded the telegram. It was a short one, and was soon done. Then I returned the code to its place, locked the safe, and then used another key on the bunch to lock a drawer in this desk. I had no occasion to go to the safe again till about 12.20, when the Controller's secretary came here with a telegram to be de-coded. The safe was still locked then, but when it was opened the code was gone."

"You had had no occasion to go to the safe in the meantime?"

"None at all. I locked it at 10.20, and I unlocked it two hours later, and that was all."

"You were not in the room the whole of the time, of course?"

"Oh, no. I have told you that at 10.20 I went to the Controller's room, and after that I went out two or three times on one occasion or another. But each time I locked the door of the room."

"Oh, you did? That is important. And you took all your keys with you, I presume?"

"Yes, all. The keys on the bunch I took in my pocket, of course, and the room door key I also took. There are one or two rather important papers on my desk, you see, and anybody from the corridor might come in if the door were left unlocked."

"The lock of the door would be a good deal easier to pick than that of the safe," Hewitt observed, after examining it. "But that would be of no great use with the safe locked. Shortly, then, the facts are these. You locked the code safely away at 10.20, you left the room two or three times, but each time the door, as well as the safe, was locked, and the keys in your pocket; and then, at 12.20, or two hours exactly after the code had been put safely away, you opened the safe again in presence of the Controller's secretary, and the code had vanished. That is the whole matter in brief, I take it?"

"Precisely." Mr. Telfer was pallid and bewildered. "It seems a total impossibility," he said; "a total, absolute, physical impossibility; but there it is."

"But as no such thing as a physical impossibility ever happens," Hewitt replied calmly, "we must look further. Now, are there any other ways into this room than by that door into the corridor? I see another door here. What is that?"

"That door has been locked for ages. The room on the other side is one like this, with a door in the corridor; it is used chiefly to store old documents of no great importance, and I believe that whole stacks of them, in bundles, are piled against the other side of that same door. We will send for the key and see, if you like."

The key was sent for, and the door from the corridor opened. As Telfer had led us to expect, the place was full of old papers in bundles and parcels, thick with ancient dust, and these things were piled high against the door next his room, and plainly had not been disturbed for months, or even years.

"There remains the skylight," said Hewitt, "for I perceive, Mr. Telfer, that your room is lighted from above, and has no window; while the grate is a register. There seems to be no opening in that skylight but the revolving ventilator. Am I right?"

"Quite so. There is no getting in by the skylight without breaking it, and, as you see, it has not been broken. Certainly there are men on the roof repairing the leads, but it is plain enough that nobody has come that way. The thing is wholly inexplicable."

"At present, yes," Hewitt said, musingly. He stood for a few moments in deep thought.

"Plummer is longer away than I expected," he said presently. "By the way, what was the external appearance of the missing code?"

"It was nothing but a sort of thin manuscript book, made of a few sheets of foolscap size, sewn in a cover of thickish grey paper. I left it in the safe doubled lengthwise, and tied with tape in the middle."

"Its loss is a very serious thing, of course?"

"Oh, terribly, terribly serious, Mr. Hewitt," Telfer replied, despairingly. "I am responsible, and it will put an end to my career, of course. But the consequences to the country are more important, and they may be disastrous—enormously so. A great sum would be paid for that code on the Continent, I need hardly say."

"But now that you know it is taken, surely the code can be changed?"

"It's not so easy as it seems, Mr. Hewitt," Telfer answered, shaking his head. "It means time, and I needn't tell you that with affairs in their present state we can't afford one moment of time. Some expedients are being attempted, of course, but you will understand that any new code would have to be arranged with scattered items of the fleet in all parts of the world, and that probably with the present code in the hands of the enemy. Moreover, all our messages already sent will be accessible with very little trouble, and they contain all our strategical coaling and storing dispositions for a great war, Mr. Hewitt; and they can't, they *can't* be altered at a moment's notice! Oh, it is terrible!... But here is Inspector Plummer. No news, I suppose, Mr. Plummer?"

"Well, no," Plummer answered deliberately. "I can't say I've any news for *you*, Mr. Telfer, just yet. But I want to talk about a few things to Mr. Hewitt. Hadn't we better go and see if your telegram is answered, Mr. Hewitt? Unless you've heard."

"No, I haven't," Hewitt replied. "We'll go on at once. Good-day for the present, Mr. Telfer. I hope to bring good news when next I see you."

"I hope so, too, Mr. Hewitt, most fervently," Telfer answered; and his looks confirmed his words.

We walked in silence through the corridor, down the stairs, and out by the gates into the street. Then Plummer turned on his heel and faced Hewitt.

"That man's a wrong 'un," he said, abruptly, jerking his thumb in the direction of the office we had just left. "I'll tell you about it in the cab."

As soon as our cab was started on its way back to Hewitt's office Plummer explained himself.

"He's been watched," he said, "has Mr. Telfer, when he didn't know it; and he'll be watched again for the rest of to-day, as I've arranged. What's more, he won't be allowed to leave the office this evening till I have seen him again, or sent a message. No need to frighten him too soon—it mightn't suit us. But he's in it, alone or in company!"

"How do you know?"

"I'll tell you. It seems the lead roofs are being repaired at the Admiralty, and the plumbers are walking about where they like. Now I needn't tell you I've had a man or two fishing about among the doorkeepers and so on at the Admiralty, and one of them found a plumber he knew slightly, working on the roof. That plumber happens to be no fool—a bit smarter than the detective-constable, it seems to me, in fact. Anyhow, he seems to have got more out of my man than my man got out of him; and soon after I reached the Yard he turned up, asking to see me. He said he'd heard that a valuable paper was missing (he didn't know what) from the room with the skylight in the top floor, where the gentleman with the single eye-glass was, and where the safe was let in the wall; and he wanted to know what would be the reward for anybody giving information about it. Of course I couldn't make any promise, and I gave him to understand that he would have to leave the amount of the reward to the authorities, if his information was worth anything; also, that we were getting to work fast, and that if he wished to be first to give information he'd better be quick about it; but I promised to make a special report of his name and what he had to say if it were useful. And it will be, or I'm vastly mistaken! For just you see here. Our friend, Mr. Telfer, says he put that code safely away at 10.20 in the safe, and that he never went to the safe again till 12.20, when the Controller's secretary was with him; never went to it for anything whatever, observe. Well, the plumber happened to be near the skylight at half-past eleven, and he is prepared to swear that he saw Mr. Telfer—'the gent with the eye-glass,' as he calls him—go to the safe, unlock it, take out a grey paper, folded lengthwise, with red tape round it, re-lock the safe, and carry that paper out into the corridor! The plumber was kneeling by a brazier, it seems, which was close by the skylight, and he is so certain of the time because he was regulating his watch by Westminster Hall clock, and compared it when the half-hour struck, which was just while Telfer was absent in the corridor with the paper. He was only gone a second or two, and you will remember that Corder saw Mayes leaving the premises within two minutes of that time!"

"Yes!"

"Well, Telfer was back in a second or two, *without the paper*, and went on with his affairs as before. That's pretty striking, eh?"

"Yes," Hewitt answered thoughtfully, "it is."

"It was a sort of shot in the dark on the part of the plumber, for he knew nothing else—nothing about Telfer legitimately having the keys of the safe, nor any of the particulars we have been told. He merely knew that a paper was missing, and having seen a paper taken out of the safe he got it into his head that he had possibly witnessed the theft; and he kept his knowledge to himself till he could see somebody in authority. Mighty keen, too, about a reward!"

"And now you are having Telfer supervised?"

"I am. Not that we're likely to get the code from him; that's passed out, sure enough, in Mayes's hands—or else his pockets."

To this confident expression of opinion Hewitt offered no reply, and presently we alighted at his office, eager to learn if Peytral had given the information Hewitt so much desired. Sure enough a telegram was there, and it ran thus:

"On the night you know of, Mayes went first to 37 Raven Street, Blackfriars, then to 8 Norbury Row, Barbican. Message follows."

"Now we're at work," Hewitt said, briskly, "and for a while we part. I shall make a few changes of dress, and go to take a look at 37 Raven Street, Blackfriars. Will you two go on to Norbury Row? You'll have to be careful, Plummer, and not show yourself. That is where Brett will be useful, since he isn't known; if anybody is to be seen let it be him. I shall be very careful myself—though I shall have some little disguise; and I fancy I shall not be so likely to be seen as you."

"What are we to do?" I asked.

"Well, of course, if you see Mayes in the open, grab him instantly. I needn't tell Plummer *that*. I think Plummer would naturally seize him on the spot, rush him off to the nearest station and go back with enough men to clear out No. 8 Norbury Row. If you don't see him you'll keep an observation, according to Plummer's discretion. But, unless some exceptional chance occurs, I hope you won't go rushing in till we communicate with each other—we must work together, and I may have news. My instinct seems to tell me that yours is the right end of the stick, at Barbican. But we must neglect nothing, and that is why I want you to hold on there while I make the necessary examination at the other end. Do you know this Norbury Row, Plummer?"

"I think I know every street and alley in the City," Plummer answered. "There is a very good publican at the corner of Norbury Row, who's been useful to the police a score of times. He keeps his eyes open, and I shall be surprised if he can't give us *some* information about No. 8, anyhow. Moon's his name, and the house is 'The Compasses.' I shall go there first. And if you've any message to send, send it through him. I'll tell him."

On the stairs Plummer and I encountered another of his assistants. "I've got the cab, sir," he reported. "Waiting outside now. Took up a fare in Whitehall, opposite the Admiralty, and drove him to Charterhouse Street; got down just by the Meat Market. That's all the man seems to know."

Plummer questioned the cabman, and found that as a matter of fact that was all he did know. So, telling him to wait to take us our little journey, we returned and reported his information to Hewitt.

"Just as I expected," he said, quietly. "He stopped the cab a bit short of his destination, of course,—just as you will, no doubt. There's not a great deal in the evidence, but it confirms my idea."

II

We followed Mayes's example by stopping the cab in Charterhouse Street, and walking the short remaining distance to Barbican. Norbury Row was an obscure street behind it, at the corner of which stood "The Compasses," the public-house which Plummer had mentioned. We did not venture to show ourselves in Norbury Row, but hastened into the nearest door of "The Compasses," which chanced to be that of the private bar.

A stout, red-faced, slow-moving man with one eye and a black patch, stood behind the bar. Plummer lifted his finger and pointed quickly toward the bar-parlour; and at the signal the one-eyed man turned with great deliberation and pulled a catch which released the door of that apartment, close at our elbows. We stepped quickly within, and presently the one-eyed man came rolling in by the other door.

"Well, good art'noon, Mr. Plummer, sir," he said, with a long intonation and a wheeze. "Good art'noon, sir. You've bin a stranger lately."

"Good afternoon, Mr. Moon," Plummer answered, briskly. "We've come for a little information, my friend and I, which I'm sure you'll give us if you can."

"All the years I've been knowed to the police," answered Mr. Moon, slower and wheezier as he went on, "I've allus give 'em all the information I could, an' that's a fact. Ain't it, Mr. Plummer?"

"Yes, of course, and we don't forget it. What we want now——"

"Allus tell 'em what—ever I knows," rumbled Mr. Moon, turning to me, "allus; an' glad to do it, too. 'Cause why? Ain't they the police? Very well then, I tells 'em. Allus tells 'em!"

Plummer waited patiently while Mr. Moon stared solemnly at me after this speech. Then, when the patch slowly turned in my direction and the eye in his, he resumed, "We want to know if you know anything about No. 8 Norbury Row?"

131

"Number eight," Mr. Moon mused, gazing abstractedly out of the window; "num—ber eight. Ground-floor, Stevens, packing-case maker; first-floor, Hutt, agent in fancy-goods; second-floor, dunno. Name o' Richardson, bookbinder, on the door, but that's bin there five or six year now, and it ain't the same tenant. Richardson's dead, an' this one don't bind no books as I can see. I don't even remember seein' him *very* often. Tallish, darkish sort o' gent he is, and don't seem to have many visitors. Well, then there's the top-floor—but I s'pose it's the same tenant. Richardson used to have it for his workshop. That's all."

"Have you got a window we can watch it from?"

Mr. Moon turned ponderously round and without a word led the way to the first floor, puffing enormously on the stairs.

"You *can* see it from the club-room," he said at length, "but this 'ere little place is better."

He pushed open a door, and we entered a small sitting-room. "That's the place," he said, pointing. "There's a new packing-case a-standing outside now."

Norbury Row presented an appearance common enough in parts of the city a little way removed from the centre. A street of houses that once had sheltered well-to-do residents had gradually sunk in the world to the condition of tenement-houses, and now was on the upward grade again, being let in floors to the smaller sort of manufacturers, and to such agents and small commercial men as required cheap offices. No. 8 was much like the rest. A packing-case maker had the ground-floor, as Moon had said, and a token of his trade, in the shape of a new packing-case, stood on the pavement. The rest of the building showed nothing distinctive.

"There y'are, gents," said Mr. Moon, "if you want to watch, you're welcome, bein' the p'lice, which I allus does my best for, allus. But you'll have to excuse me now, 'cos o' the bar."

Mr. Moon stumped off downstairs, leaving Plummer and myself watching at the window.

"Your friend the publican seems very proud of helping the police," I remarked.

Plummer laughed. "Yes," he said, "or at any rate, he is anxious we shan't forget it. You see, it's in some way a matter of mutual accommodation. We make things as easy as possible for him on licensing days, and as he has a pretty extensive acquaintance among the sort of people we often want to get hold of, he has been able to show his gratitude very handsomely once or twice."

The house on which our eyes were fixed was a little too far up the street for us to see perfectly through the window of the second-floor, though we could see enough to indicate that it was furnished as an office. We agreed that the unknown second-floor tenant was more likely to be our customer, or connected with him, than either of the others. Still, we much desired a nearer view, and presently, since the coast seemed clear, Plummer announced his intention of taking one.

He left me at the post of observation, and presently I saw him lounging along on the other side of the way, keeping close to the houses, so as to escape observation from the upper windows. He took a good look at the names on the door-post of No. 8, and presently stepped within.

I waited five or six minutes, and then saw him returning as he had come.

"It's the top floors we want," he said, when he rejoined me in Mr. Moon's sitting-room. "The packing-case maker is genuine enough, and very busy. So is the fancy-goods agent. I went in, seeing the door wide open, and found the agent, a little, shop-walkery sort of chap, hard at work with his clerk among piles of cardboard boxes. I wouldn't go further, in case I were spotted. Do you think you'd be cool enough to do it without arousing suspicion? Mayes doesn't know you, you see. What do you think? We don't want to precipitate matters till we hear from Hewitt, but on the other hand I don't want to sit still as long as anything can be ascertained. You might ask a question about book-binding."

"Of course," I said. "If you will let me I'll go at once—glad of the chance to get a peep. I'll bespeak a quotation for binding and lettering a thousand octavos in paste grain, on behalf of some convenient firm of publishers. That would be technical enough, I think?"

I took my hat and walked out as Plummer had done, though, of course, I approached the door of No. 8 with less caution. The packing-case maker's men were hammering away merrily, and as I mounted the stairs I saw the little fancy-goods agent among his cardboard boxes, just as Plummer had said. The upper part of the house was a silent contrast to the busy lower floors, and as I arrived at the next landing I was surprised to see the door ajar.

I pushed boldly in, and found myself alone in a good-sized room plainly fitted as an office. There were two windows looking on the street, and one at the back, more than half concealed behind a ground glass partition or screen. I stepped across and looked out of this window. It looked on a narrow space, or well, of plain brick wall, containing nothing but a ladder, standing in one corner. And the only other window giving on this narrow square space was in the opposite wall, but much lower, on the ground level.

I saw these things in a single glance, and then I turned—to find myself face to face with a tallish, thin, active man, with a pale, shaven, ascetic face, dark hair, and astonishingly quick glittering black eyes. He stood just within the office door, to which he must have come without a sound, looking at me with a mechanical smile of inquiry, while his eyes searched me with a portentous keenness.

"Oh," I said, with the best assumption of carelessness I could command, "I was looking for you, Mr. Richardson. Do you care to give a quotation for binding at per thousand crown octavo volumes in paste grain, plain, with lettering on back?"

"No," answered the man with the eyes, "I don't; I'm afraid my carelessness has led you into a mistake. I am not Richardson the bookbinder. He was my predecessor in this office, and I have neglected to paint out his name on the door-post."

I hastened to apologise. "I am sorry to have intruded," I said. "I found the door ajar and so came in. You see the publishing season is beginning, and our regular binders are full of work, so that we have to look elsewhere. Good-day!"

"Good-day," the keen man responded, turning to allow me to pass through the door. "I'm sorry I cannot be of service to you—on this occasion."

From first to last his eyes had never ceased to search me, and now as I descended the stairs I could *feel* that they were fixed on me still.

I took a turn about the houses, in order not to be observed going direct to "The Compasses," and entered that house by way of the private bar, as before.

"That is Mayes, and no other," said Plummer, when I had made my report and described the man with the eyes. "I've seen him twice, once with his beard and once without. The question now is, whether we hadn't best sail in straight away and collar him. But there's the window at the back, and a ladder, I think you said. Can he reach it?"

"I think he might—easily."

"And perhaps there's the roof, since he's got the top floor too. Not good enough without some men to surround the house. We must go gingerly over this. One thing to find out is, what is the building behind? Ah, how I wish Mr. Hewitt were here now! If we don't hear from him soon we must send a message. But we mustn't lose sight of No. 8 for a moment."

There was a thump at the sitting-room door, and Mr. Moon came puffing in and shouldered himself confidentially against Plummer. "Bloke downstairs wants to see you," he said, in a hoarse grunt that was meant for a low whisper. "Twigged you outside, I think, an' says he's got somethink partickler to tell yer. I believe 'e's a 'nark'; I see him with one o' your chaps the other day."

"I'll go," Plummer said to me hurriedly. "Plainly somebody's spotted me in the street, and I may as well hear him."

I knew very well, of course, what Moon meant by a 'nark.' A 'nark' is an informer, a spy among criminals who sells the police whatever information he can scrape up. Could it be possible that this man had anything to tell about Mayes? It was scarcely likely, and I made up my mind that Plummer was merely being detained by some tale of a petty local crime.

But in a few minutes he returned with news of import. "This fellow is most valuable," he said. "He knows a lot about Mayes, whom, of course, he calls by another name; but the identity's certain. He saw me looking in at No. 8, he says, and guessed I must be after him. He seems to have wondered at Mayes's mysterious movements for a long time, and so kept his eye on him and made inquiries. It seems that Mayes sometimes uses a back way, through the window you saw on the opposite side of the little area, by way of that ladder you mentioned. It's quite plain this fellow knows something, from the particulars about that ladder. He wants half a sovereign to show me the way through a stable passage behind and point out where our man can be trapped to a certainty. It'll be a cheap ten shillingsworth, and we mustn't waste time. If Hewitt comes, tell him not to move till I come back or send a message, which I can easily do by this chap I'm going with. And be sure to keep your eye on the front door of No. 8 while I'm gone."

The thing had begun to grow exciting, and the fascination of the pursuit took full possession of my imagination. I saw Plummer pass across the end of the street in company with a shuffling, out-at-elbows-looking man with dirty brown whiskers, and I set myself to watch the door of the staircase by the packing-case maker's with redoubled attention, hoping fervently that Mayes might emerge, and so give me the opportunity of capping the extraordinary series of occurrences connected with the Red Triangle by myself seizing and handing him over to the police.

So I waited and watched for something near another quarter of an hour. Then there came another thump at the door, and once more I beheld Mr. Moon.

"Man askin' for you in the bar, sir," he said.

"Asking for me?" I asked, a little astonished. "By name?"

"Mr. Brett, 'e said, sir. He's the same chap, you know. He's got a message from Inspector Plummer, 'e says."

"May he come up here?" I asked, mindful of maintaining my watch.

"Certainly, sir, if you like. I'll bring him."

Presently the shuffling man with the dirty whiskers presented himself. He was a shifty, villainous-looking fellow of middle height, looking a "nark" all over. He pulled off his cap and delivered his message in a rum-scented whisper. "Inspector Plummer says the front way don't matter now," he said. "'E can cop 'im fair the other way if you'll go round to him at once. If Mr. Martin Hewitt's here 'e'd rather 'ave 'im, but on'y one's to come now."

Naturally, I thought, Plummer would prefer Hewitt; but in this case I should for once be ahead of my friend, and have the pleasure of relating the circumstances of the capture to him, instead of listening, as usual, to his own quiet explanations of the manner in which the case had been brought to a successful issue. So I took my hat and went.

"Best let me go in front," whispered the "nark." "You bein' a toff might be noticed." It was a reasonable precaution, and I followed him accordingly.

We went a little way down Barbican, and presently, taking a very narrow turning, plunged into a cluster of alleys, through which, however, I could plainly perceive that our way lay in the direction of the back of the house in Norbury Row. At length my guide stopped at what seemed a stable yard, pushed open a wicket gate, and went in, keeping the gate open for me to follow.

It was, indeed, a stable yard, littered with much straw, which the "nark" carefully picked to walk on as noiselessly as possible, motioning me to do the same. It was a small enough yard, and dark, and when my guide very carefully opened the door of a stable I saw that that was darker still.

He pushed the door wide so as to let a little light fall on another door which I now perceived in the brick wall which formed the side of the stable. After listening intently for a moment at this door, the guide stepped back and favoured me with another puff of rum and a whisper. "There's no light in that there passage," he said, "an' we'd better not strike one. I'll catch hold of your hand."

He pulled the stable door to, and took me by the hand. I heard the inner door open quietly, and we stepped cautiously forward. We had gone some five or six yards in the darkness when I felt something cold touch the wrist of the hand by which I was being led. There was a loud click, my hand was dropped, and I felt my wrist held fast, while I could hear my late guide shuffling away in the darkness.

I could not guess whether to cry out or remain quiet. I called after the man in a loud whisper, but got no answer. I used my other hand to feel at my right wrist, and found that it was clipped in one of a pair of handcuffs, the other being locked in a staple in the wall. I tugged my hardest to loosen this staple, but it held firm. The thing had been so sudden and stealthy that I scarce had time to realise that I was in serious danger, and that, doubtless, Plummer had preceded me, when a light appeared at an angle ahead. It turned the corner, and I perceived, coming toward me, carrying a lamp, the pale man of the eyes, whom I had encountered not an hour before—in a word, Mayes.

His eyes searched me still, but he approached me with a curiously polite smile.

"No, Mr. Brett," he said, "my name is not Richardson, and I am not a bookbinder. Not that I am particular about such a thing as a name, for you have heard of me under more than one already, and you are quite at liberty to call me Richardson if you like. I am sorry to have to talk to you in this uncomfortable place, but the circumstances are exceptional. But, at least, I should give you a chair."

He stepped back a little way and pressed a bell-button. Presently the fellow who had decoyed me there appeared, and Mayes ordered him to bring me a chair at once, which he did, with stolid obedience. I sat in it, so that my wrist rested at somewhere near the level of my shoulder.

"Mr. Brett," Mayes pursued, when his man was gone, "I am not so implacable a person as you perhaps believe me; in fact, I can assure you that my disposition is most friendly."

"Then unfasten this handcuff," I said.

"I am sorry that that is a little precaution I find it necessary to take till we understand each other better. I am glad to see you, Mr. Brett, though I am sure you will not think me rude if I say that I should have preferred Mr. Martin Hewitt in your place. But perhaps his turn will come later. I have a proposition to make, Mr. Brett. I should like you to join me."

"To join you?"

"Exactly." He nodded pleasantly. "You needn't shrink; I shan't ask you to do anything vulgar, or even anything that, with your present prejudices, you might consider actively criminal. You can help me, you see, in your own profession as a journalist; and in other ways. And my enterprise is greater than you may imagine. Join me, and you shall be a great man in an entirely new sphere. A small matter of initiation is necessary, and that is all. You have only to consent to that."

I said nothing.

"You seem reluctant. Well, perhaps it is natural, in your present ignorance. This is no vulgar criminal organisation that I have, understand. I have taken certain measures to provide myself with the necessary tools in the shape of money, and so forth, but my aims are larger than you suspect—perhaps larger than you can understand. And I work with a means more wonderful than you have experience of. For instance, here is to-day's work. You know about the lost Naval Code, of course—it is what you came about. That document is now lying in the desk you stood by in the room where we spoke of paste grain book covers and the like. It was there then at your elbow. It will be sold for many thousands of pounds by to-morrow, and all the puny watchings and dodgings that have been devised cannot prevent it. The money will go to aid me in the attainment of the power of which you may have a part, if you wish. The means of attaining this I scruple no more about than you did to-day about the story of the bookbindings." He bowed with a slight smile and went on.

"Come now, Mr. Brett, put aside your bourgeois prejudices and join me. Your friend Plummer is coming gladly, I feel sure, and he will be useful, too. And from what I have seen from Mr. Martin Hewitt, I have no doubt I can make it right with him. If I can't it will be very bad for him, I can assure you; you have heard and seen something of my powers, and I need say no more. But Hewitt is a man of sense, and will come in, of course, and you had better come with your friends. I want one or two superior men. Mason—you know about Jacob Mason, of course—Mason was a fool, and he was lost— inevitably. The others"—he made a gesture of contempt—"they are mere vulgar tools. They will have their rewards if they are faithful, of course; if not—well, you remember Denson in the Samuel diamond business? He was *not* faithful, and there was an end of him. I may tell you that Denson was made an example, for one was needed. I assigned him a certain operation, and, having brought it to success, he endeavoured to embezzle—did embezzle—the proceeds. He was made a conspicuous example, in a most conspicuous public place, to impress the others. They didn't know *him*, but they knew well enough what the Red Triangle meant! Ah, my excellent recruit—for so I count you already—there is more in that little sign than you can imagine! It is more than a sign—it is an implement of very potent power; and you shall learn its whole secret in that little form of initiation I spoke of. See now, a present example. Telfer, the Admiralty clerk, gave up that document at my mere spoken word. He will deny it to his dying day, and he will be ruined for the act; but he gave me the paper himself, at my mere order. If he were one of my own—if he had passed through the initiation I offer you, I would have protected him; as it is, he must take his punishment, and though it is only I who will benefit, he will still deny the fact! Ha! Mr. Brett, do you begin to perceive that I do not boast when I tell of powers beyond your understanding?"

Truly I was amazed, though I could not half understand. The circumstances of the loss of the Admiralty code had been so inexplicable, and now these incredible suggestions of the prime actor in the matter were more mysterious still.

"Ha! you are amazed," he went on, "but if you will come further into my counsels I will amaze you more. What are you now? A drudge of a journalist, and if ever you make a thousand a year to feed yourself with you will be lucky. Come to me and you shall be a man of power. There is a place beyond the sea where I may be king, and you a viceroy. Don't think I am raving! It is true enough that I am an enthusiast, but I have power, power to do anything I please, I tell you! What are the greatest powers among men on this earth? Some will say the pen, or the sword, or love, or what not. Men of the world will say, money and lies; and they will be very nearly right. Money and lies will move continents, but I have one greater power still—the very apex of the triangle! That power I revealed to Jacob Mason. He thought to betray it, and it killed him. That power I will reveal to you, if you will accept the alternative I offer."

"The alternative?"

"Yes, the alternative, for an alternative it is, of course. If you will go through the form of initiation, I shall keep you here a little till I can trust you—which will be very soon. But if not—well, Mr. Brett, I wish to be as friendly as you please, but having been at the trouble of catching you, and having got you here safely, you who know so much now, you who could be so dangerous if you ever got away— eh? Well, you know my methods, and you have seen them exemplified, and you will understand."

There was no anger in his voice as he uttered this threat, nor even, I thought, in his eyes. But what there was was worse.

"But I'm sure you will not make things unpleasant," he concluded. "You will go through the little form I have arranged, if only for curiosity. Just think over it for a moment, while I go to close my little office."

He took the lamp and turned away, but as he reached the angle of the passage, there came a sound that checked his steps. I could hear a noise of feet and hurried voices, and then suddenly arose a shout in a voice which seemed to be Plummer's. "Here!" it cried. "Help! This way, Hewitt! Brett!"

I shouted back at the top of my voice, wondering where Plummer was, and what it might all mean. And with that Mayes turned, and I saw that he was about to make for the door I had entered by. I resolved he should not pass me if I could prevent it, and I sprang up and seized my chair in my left hand, shouting aloud for help as I did so.

Mayes came with a bound, and flung his lighted lamp full at my head. It struck the chair and smashed to a thousand pieces, and in that instant of time Mayes was on me. Plainly he had no weapon, or he would have used it; but I was at disadvantage enough, with my right wrist chained to the wall. I clung with all my might, and endeavoured to swing my enemy round against the wall in order that I might clasp my hands about him, and I shouted my loudest as I did it. But the chair and the broken glass hampered me, and Mayes was desperate. The agony in my right wrist was unbearable, and just as I was conscious of a rush of approaching feet a heavy blow took me full in the face, and I felt Mayes rush over me while I fell and hung from the wrist.

I had a stunned sense of lights and voices and general confusion, and then I remembered nothing.

III

I came to myself on the floor of a lighted room, with Hewitt's face over mine. My wrist seemed broken, though it was free, there was oil and blood on my clothes, and in my left hand I still gripped a piece of Mayes's coat.

"Stop him!" I cried. "He's gone by the stable! Have they got him?"

"No good, Brett," Hewitt answered soberly. "You did your best, but he's gone, and Peytral after him!"

"Peytral?"

"Yes. He brought his own message to town. But see if you can stand up."

I was well enough able to do that, and, indeed, I had only fainted from the pain of the strain on my wrist. Several policemen were in the room, beside Hewitt and Plummer. Mayes's stronghold was in the hands of his enemies.

Then I suddenly remembered.

"The Admiralty code!" I cried. "It was in the office desk. Have you got it?"

"No," Hewitt answered. "Come, Plummer, up the ladder!"

Little time was lost in forcing Mayes's desk, and there the document was found, grey cover, red tape and all intact. The police were left to make a vigorous search for any possible copy, and the original was handed to Plummer, as chief representative of the law present. He had been trapped precisely as I had been, except that he had been led further, and shut in a cellar as well as fastened by the wrist. Mayes, it seemed, had wasted very little time in attempting to pervert him, and I have no doubt that, whatever fate might have been reserved for me, Plummer would never have left the place alive had it not been for the timely irruption of Hewitt, with Peytral and the police.

In half an hour Peytral returned. He had dashed out in chase of the fugitive, but failed even to see him—lost him wholly in the courts, in fact. For some little while he persevered, but found it useless.

The dirty-whiskered man made no attempt to escape, though there was talk of another man having got away in the confusion by way of the stable roof. The police were left in charge of the place, and we deferred a complete exploration till the next day.

Hewitt's tale was simple enough. He had endued himself in somewhat seedy clothes, and had visited 37 Raven Street, Blackfriars, which he found to be merely a tenement house. It took some time to make inquiries there, with the necessary caution, because of the number of lodgers; and then the inquiries led to nothing. It was an experience common enough in his practice, but none the less an annoying delay, and when he returned to his office he found Mr. Peytral already awaiting him. Peytral described his following of Mayes at much greater length and detail than before, and he and Hewitt had come on to Norbury Row at once and asked news of Mr. Moon.

Mr. Moon's description of the successive disappearances of Plummer and myself, and of our continued absence, so aroused Hewitt's suspicions that he instantly procured help from the nearest station, and approached the door of Mayes's office. A knock being unanswered, the door was instantly broken in. The room was found to be unoccupied, but the ladder was still standing at the open window, by which Mayes had descended to the back premises. Down this ladder Hewitt went, with the police after him. The rest I had seen myself.

"But what," I said, "what is this mystery? Why did Telfer give up the code, and what is the power that Mayes talks of?"

"It is a power," replied Hewitt, "that I have suspected for some time, and now I am quite sure of it. A secret, dangerous and terrible power which I have encountered before, though never before have I known its possibilities carried so far. It is hypnotism!"

"Hypnotism!" I exclaimed. "But can a person be hypnotised against his will?"

"In a sense, in most cases, he cannot. That is the explanation of Mayes's proposals to you to go through a 'form of initiation.' If you had consented, the 'form' would have been a process of hypnotism. Once or twice repeated, and you would have been wholly under his control, so that if he willed it and forbade you, you could tell nothing of what he wished kept secret, and you would have committed any crime he might suggest. Consider poor Jacob Mason! Remember how he struggled to tell what he knew, oppressed by the horror of it, and how it all ended! And remember Henning the clerk, Mayes's tool in that case of bond robbery! What has happened to him? He committed suicide, as you know, immediately after Mayes had left him at the barn. Brett, this power of hypnotism, a power for healing in the hands of a good man, may become a terrible power for evil in the hands of a villain!"

"But Telfer, to-day? He seems to have known nothing of Mayes, and he was not one of his regular creatures—Mayes himself told me so."

"About that I don't know. But I expect we shall find that he has been willingly hypnotised at some time or another, perhaps more than once, by this same scoundrel Mayes. Possibly in one of Mayes's appearances in respectable society, at an evening party, or the like. In a case of that sort the hypnotist may impress a certain formula—a word, a name, or a number—on the subject's mind, by the repetition of which, at any future time, that same subject may be instantly hypnotised. So that, once having become hypnotised, on any innocent occasion, the subject is in the power of the hypnotist, more or less, ever after. The hypnotist says: 'When I repeat such and such a sentence or number to you in future, you will be hypnotised,' and hypnotised the subject duly is, instantly. Supposing such a case in this matter of Mr. Telfer, it would only be necessary for Mayes to meet him in the corridor, repeat his formula and command the victim to bring out the paper he specified. This done he could similarly order him to *forget the whole transaction,* and this the victim would do, infallibly."

It is only necessary to say here, parenthetically, that later inquiry proved the truth of Hewitt's supposition. Twice or three times Mr. Telfer had been hypnotised in a friend's chambers, by a plausible tall man whose acquaintance his host had made at some public scientific gathering. And in the end it became possible to identify this man with Mayes.

Mr. Moon, of "The Compasses," was of great comfort to me that evening. My cuts and bruises were washed in his house, and my inner man revived with his food and drink.

"Allus glad to oblige the p'lice," said Mr. Moon; "allus. 'Cos why? Ain't they the p'lice? Very well then!"

THE ADVENTURE OF CHANNEL MARSH

I

Mayes's stronghold was taken, but Mayes had escaped us once again; the cage was in our hands, but the bird had flown.

Martin Hewitt, however, had his plans, as he was soon to show. The recovery of the Admiralty code was a good stroke, and was a satisfactory ending to an important case; but that, and even the capture of the curious premises behind the Barbican, made but a halting-place in his pursuit of Mayes, and as soon as I was in some degree recovered from my struggle, and the captured place had been hastily searched, the chase was resumed without a moment's delay; and that adventure was entered upon which saw the end of the Red Triangle and its unholy doings—which came terribly near to seeing the end of Hewitt himself, in fact.

I have not described the den near the Barbican with any great particularity, but I have said that the office, accessible from the open street, was only connected with the hidden premises behind— premises, as was afterwards discovered, held under a separate tenancy—by an easily-shifted ladder. It was in these hidden premises, approached by the maze of courts and the stable-yard, that the main evidences of Mayes's way of life were observable. The passage where my wrist had been locked to the wall, and the room or cellar in which Plummer had been confined, were the only parts of the lower premises fitted for the detention of prisoners, with the exception of one very low and wholly unlighted cellar, entered by a trapdoor and a very steep flight of brick steps. This place smelt horribly faint and stagnant; but it produced on my mind, both then and when I examined it later, an effect of horror and repulsion more than could be accounted for by the smell alone. Of its history nothing was discovered, and perhaps the feeling (though others experienced it as well as myself) was the effect of mere fancy; but I have never got rid of a conviction that that black cellar, or rather pit—for it was very narrow—had been the instrument of crimes never to be told.

There were one or two rooms sparely furnished—one as a bedroom, a larger room, with a long table, a sofa, and several chairs; and in one of the smaller rooms was found a stove, ladles and crucibles for the melting down of metals—gold or silver. It was in this same room also that the table stood, in the drawers of which were found papers, letters and formulæ—things giving more than a hint of the use to which Mayes had put his friendship with Mr. Jacob Mason, for of every possible manner and detail in which science—more particularly the science of chemistry—could aid in the commission of crime, there were notes in these same drawers.

But most of these things were observed in detail later. The thing that set us once more on the trail of Mayes, that very night and that very hour, was found in the isolated office facing the street. It was a cheque-book, quite full of unused cheques.

"This cheque-book," said Hewitt to Inspector Plummer and myself, "was in the drawer below that in which we discovered the Admiralty code. The Eastern Consolidated is the bank, as you see— Upper Holloway branch. Now we must follow this at once, before waiting to search any further. There may be something more important as a clue, or there may not, but at any rate, while we are looking for it we are losing time. This may bring us to him at once."

"You mean that he may have some address in Holloway," suggested Plummer, "and we may get it from the bank?"

"There's that possibility, and another," Hewitt answered. "He has had to bolt without warning or preparation, with nothing but the clothes he ran in—probably very little money. Money he will want at once, and he would rather not wait till the morning to get it; if he can get it at once it will mean thirteen or fourteen hours' start at least. More, he will know very well that this place will be searched, that this cheque-book will be discovered soon enough, and that consequently the bank will be watched. This is what he will do— what he is doing now, very likely. He will knock up the resident manager of that bank and try to get a cheque cashed to-night. I don't think that can be done; in which case he will probably try to make some arrangement to have money sent him. Either way, we must be at the Upper Holloway branch of the Eastern Consolidated Bank as soon as a hansom can get us there."

Thus it was settled, and Hewitt and Plummer went off at once, leaving Plummer's men, with the City police, in charge of the raided premises; leaving some of them also to make inquiries in the neighbourhood. Mr. Victor Peytral had shown himself anxious to accompany Hewitt and Plummer, but had been dissuaded by Hewitt. I guessed that Hewitt feared that some hasty indiscretion on the part of this terribly wronged man might endanger his plans. Peytral, however, seemed tractable enough, and left immediately after them; he had business, he said, which he expected would occupy him for a day or two, and when it was completed he would see us again.

As for myself I only remained long enough to ascertain that the police could find no trace of the direction of Mayes's flight in the immediate neighbourhood. They had little to aid them. He had gone without a hat, and his dress was in some degree disordered by his struggle with me; but the latter defect he might easily have remedied in the courts as he ran, and they could gather no tidings of a hatless man. So I took my way to my office, my wrist growing stiffer and more painful as I went, so that I was not sorry to arrange for another member of the staff to take my duty for the night, and to get to bed a few hours earlier than usual, after the day's fatigue and excitement.

II

Going to bed uncommonly soon I woke correspondingly early in the morning; but I was no earlier than Hewitt, who was at my door, in fact, ere my breakfast was well begun.

"Well," I asked eagerly, almost before my friend had entered, "have you got him at last?"

"Not yet," Hewitt answered. "But he did exactly as I had expected. Plummer and I knocked up the bank manager, who lives over the premises at the Upper Holloway branch. He was a very decent fellow—rather young for the post—but he was naturally a bit surprised, possibly irritated, at being bothered by one and another after office hours. I showed him the cheque-book, and asked him if it belonged to any customer of his.

"'Why, yes,' he said, examining the numbers, 'I remember this because it is the first of a new series, and we issued it the day before yesterday to a new customer. Where did you get it?'

"'We are very anxious to see that customer,' I said. 'Has he been here this evening?'

"The manager seemed a trifle surprised, but answered readily enough. 'Yes,' he said, 'he was here not an hour ago.'

"'Wanting to draw money?' I asked. But that the manager wouldn't tell me, of course. So that it was necessary for Plummer to step in and reveal the facts that this was a police matter, and that he was a detective-inspector. That made some difference. The manager told us that our man had opened an account at the bank only two days before; and I'd like you to guess what name he had opened it under."

"Not Myatt?" I said. "After the chase——"

"No, not Myatt."

"Catherton Hunt?"

"No, nor Catherton Hunt. He had opened it in the name of Mayes!"

"What! his actual name?"

"His actual original name, according to Peytral. The account was transferred, it would seem, from another bank; and I have an idea we may find that he has been shifting his money about from one bank to another as safety suggested, using his real name with it. You remember we could find no trace of a banking account when the police raided and ransacked Calton Lodge after Mason was killed? Quite probably he has had small current accounts in other names at various times to aid in his schemes, but his main account has always stood in his real name; and by that, you see, we get some confirmation of Peytral's story. Well, as I say, the account was opened in the name of Mayes, and the cheque-book was issued which we discovered last night. The Upper Holloway branch saw no more of its customer till yesterday evening, long after hours, when he drove up in a hansom."

"Oh," I said, "in a hansom, was it? The men left behind could get no news of him."

"Yes, we ascertained that last night; we called back, of course, the last thing. I expect he got the first cab visible and drove off to a hatter's a fair distance away, and then on to the bank. At any rate, he knocked up the manager and told him that he had a sudden need for money that very night; could he have some?

"The manager told him it would be impossible. Even if he had been willing to do it, against all regulations, it would still be impossible. For the strong-room and every cash receptacle in it was locked with two separate locks with different keys, and though he had one of these keys himself, it was useless without the other, which was in the possession of his second in command, who lived some distance out of London. This course is the usual precaution adopted in branch banks of this sort; opening and closing, morning and evening, have to be done by chief and assistant together. And I tell you, Brett, I believe that it was only the being informed of this fact that prevented Mayes from trying some of his hypnotic tricks on the bank manager;

in which case there would have been a big bank robbery—perhaps something worse in addition."

"Murder?"

"Murder with a tourniquet, perhaps—perhaps with some other weapon; but, at any rate, probably with the Red Triangle. You know, of course—indeed I told you, I think—that in most cases—not all—it is necessary to get the subject's consent to the *first* exercise of hypnotism on him. I told you also it is possible for the practised hypnotist, while the subject is under the influence of the *first* experiment, to suggest to him a certain word or formula, or even a silent sign, which shall bring him under the influence at any other time, whenever the hypnotist chooses to repeat it—just as must have been done with Mr. Telfer, in the case of the Admiralty code. The first suggestion would not be the difficult thing it might seem—it would only require a little time and persuasion. Nothing would be said about hypnotism, of course; perhaps something about a little physical experiment, or the like, and then in a moment or two the subject would be in this creature's power for ever. Remember the little 'ceremony of initiation' that the scoundrel attempted to persuade you to submit to! That meant hypnotism—perhaps death.

"But this is mere speculation. Mayes found that the keys on the premises were not enough to release his money, even if the strict rules of the bank had permitted the cashing of a cheque out of hours. But the manager suggested that perhaps some neighbouring tradesman would exchange cash for a cheque, and, with the view of obliging the new customer, went with him as far as the shop of Mr. Isaac Trenaman, a grocer and cheesemonger with a rather large shop at the corner of the road. Mr. Trenaman, introduced and assured by the manager, was willing to give as much cash as he could find in the till against Mr. Mayes's cheque, and did so to the extent of twenty-seven pounds, a cheque for which sum was duly drawn on one of the tradesman's own cheque forms, and left with him. This done, the bank's new customer took himself off, with thanks and apologies; carrying with him, however, two blank cheque forms from Mr. Trenaman's book, the pennies for which he punctiliously paid over the counter. Having no cheque forms with him, he explained, he might find them useful if he could come across some friend who could provide the cash he wished to use that night. And having completed this business so far, this charming new customer of the bank made off into the night."

"And is that all you know of his movements?"

"Yes, as yet. He seems to have made no very definite excuse to the manager for wanting the money in such a hurry—just said something had occurred which made cash necessary, and was very polite and apologetic, generally. The manager formed a notion that it must be for some gambling purpose—he fancied that Mayes said something distantly alluding to that, but wasn't sure."

"Did you ask about the address given to the bank?"

"Of course; but there we gained nothing. The manager couldn't remember it exactly, and the books, of course, were locked up. But we know it already—for what the manager *could* remember was that it was an office address, and somewhere near Barbican! So that we are back at the Barbican den again, where I am going now, with Plummer, to give a day to a minute investigation of the whole place. Meanwhile a watch is being set at the bank in Holloway."

"Do you expect him back there, then?"

"Hardly. You see he knows that by this time we must have found his cheque-book, and will be on the watch. But there is just a chance—a very remote one—that he may send a message; perhaps send somebody to cash a cheque. Though I don't expect it, for he is no fool—he is, indeed, a sort of genius—and that would be a mistake, I think. Still, he is bold, and that is where his money is, and he may make a dash at it. So a couple of Plummer's men are to be waiting there, this morning, in the manager's office, and if anybody comes from Mayes he will be detained. Perhaps you would like to be with them? You can't be of much use with me, and the job will be dull. But there you *may* have a chance of excitement, and you will be useful to come and report if anything does happen. Why, you may even bag Mayes himself!"

"Of course—I'll go anywhere you please. They told you last night, I suppose, that Peytral had business, and had gone off?"

"Yes, and I'm not sorry. He is too dangerous a man to have about us, with his hot blood and the terrible injuries he keeps in memory. As likely as not, if we get Mayes, we should next have to collar Peytral for shooting him, or something. So I'm not sorry he is out of it for a bit. But can you start now? Plummer is in my office and the two men are in a cab outside. The bank opens at nine, and that is in Upper Holloway."

I seized my hat and made ready.

"You should keep your eyes open," Hewitt hinted, "before you get to the bank and when you leave, as well as while you're there. Do you remember how poor Mason was watched? Well, there is probably some watching going on now. Last night, on our way to the bank and back, I believe Plummer and I were watched pretty closely."

III

Plummer's two plain-clothes men and I reached the neighbourhood of the bank with a quarter of an hour to spare, or rather more. We dismissed the cab at some little distance from the spot, and approached singly, so that it was not difficult for us to slip in separately among the dozen or fifteen clerks as they arrived. We passed directly into the manager's room, the door of which opened into the space left for the public before the counter. From this room the whole of the outer office was visible through the glass of the partition. The manager, Mr. Blockley, a quick, intelligent man of thirty-six or so, gave us chairs and pointed out how best we could watch the counter without ourselves being observed.

"If a letter is sent," he said, "it will be brought here to me, of course, and I will bring the messenger in. If a cheque is presented from Mayes, I have told the cashier to slide that big ledger off his desk accidentally with his elbow. That will be your signal, and then you can do whatever you think proper. I don't think I can do any more than that."

We took our positions and waited. I felt pretty sure that if Mayes sent at all it would be early, for obvious reasons. And I was right, for the very first customer was our man.

He stepped in briskly scarcely a minute after the manager had ceased speaking, and I remembered having seen him waiting at the street corner as I came along. He was a well-dressed, smart enough looking man, in frock coat and tall hat. He took a letter-case from his pocket, picked out a cheque from the rest of the papers in it, and passed it under the wire grille of the counter.

The cashier took it, turned it over, and shifted mechanically to post the amount in the book on his desk. As he did so his elbow touched the heavy ledger which the manager had pointed out to us, and it fell with a crash. The cashier calmly put his pen behind his ear, and stooped to pick up the book, but even as he did it the two Scotland Yard men were out before the counter, and had sidled up to the stranger, one on each side.

"May we see that cheque, if you please?" asked one, and the cashier turned its face toward him. "Ah, just so; a hundred pounds—Mayes. We must just trouble you to come with us, if you please. There is some explanation wanted about that cheque."

I had followed the two men from the manager's room, and now I saw that while one had laid his hand on the stranger's shoulder the other had taken him by the opposite arm. "Why," said the former, looking into his face, "it's Broady Sims!"

"All right," the man growled resignedly. "It's a cop. I'll go quiet."

But as he spoke I saw the free hand steal out behind him and pitch away a crumpled fragment of paper. One of the policemen saw it too, followed it with his eyes, and saw me snatch it up.

"That's right, sir," he said, "take care of that; and we'll have a cab, in case anything else drops accidentally. It's just a turning over, Broady, that's what it is."

I spread out the piece of paper, and was astonished to find inscribed on it just such another series of figures, in groups of eight, as was found in the cypher message in the Case of the Lever Key.

Here was a great find—a secret message as clear to me as to Mayes himself, and as likely as not the scrap of paper that would hang him! I took one of the plain-clothes men aside while the other kept his hold of Broady Sims.

"This is very important," I said. "It is a cypher message which Mr. Hewitt can read—or I, myself, in fact, with a little time. Must you take it with you? If so, I'll make a copy now."

"Well, sir, we're responsible, you see," the man said, "so I think we must take it; so perhaps you'd better make a copy, as you suggest."

"Very well," I said, "that is done in a few seconds. You can take your man off, and I will go direct to Mr. Hewitt and Inspector Plummer with the copy." And with that I made the copy, which read thus:—

23, 19, 15, 1, 9, 14, 9, 2; 20, 8, 1,
20, 14, 14, 20, 8; 14, 5, 12, 4, 9, 7,
5, 14; 3, 8, 18, 23, 0, 14, 1, 8; 22,
9, 6, 1, 18, 3, 5, 1; 19, 14, 15, 21,
9, 0, 20, 12; 18, 12, 21, 1, 6, 23, 20,
12; 9, 18, 15, 5, 18, 13, 12, 20.

It struck me to ask the manager if the cheque just presented were one of those procured from Mr. Trenaman the night before, and I found that it was. Then I left the policemen with their prisoner and made for the nearest cab-rank. This cypher message, no doubt conveying Mayes's instructions to the man just captured, was probably of the utmost importance, and Hewitt must see it at once; and as the cab ambled along towards Barbican I busied myself in deciphering the figures according to the plan of the knight's move in chess, as Hewitt had explained to me. I could only see two noughts among the numbers, so plainly it was a longer message than the one then deciphered—one of sixty-two letters, in fact. I turned the figures into the letters corresponding in the alphabet, *a* for 1, *b* for 2, and so on, as Hewitt had done, and I arranged these letters in the squares of a roughly drawn chessboard, so that they stood thus:—

w	s	o	a	i	n	i	b
t	h	a	t	n	n	t	h
n	e	l	d	i	g	e	n
c	h	r	w	o	n	a	h
v	i	f	a	r	c	e	a
s	n	o	u	i	o	t	l
r	l	u	a	f	w	t	l
i	r	o	e	r	m	l	t

The letters thus set out, to read off the message was a simple task enough, in view of the key Hewitt had given me. I began, as in the case of the Lever Key message, at the right-hand top corner, and taking the knight's move from *b* to *e* in the last square but one of the third line, thence to *a* at the end of the fifth line, and so to *t* in the seventh line, and from that to *r* (fifth square in bottom line), *u* in seventh line and so on, in the order shown by the Lever Key message, a copy of which I kept as a curiosity in my pocket-book. So I read the message through, and I set it down thus:—

Be at ruin Channel Marsh to-night twelve; wait in hall for instruc. Word final.

The general meaning of this seemed clear enough. The man whom the policeman had recognised as Broady Sims was to be at some spot—a ruined building, it would seem—in a place called Channel Marsh, at midnight, there to wait in the hall for instructions; no doubt for instructions where to take the hundred pounds he was to have got from the bank. "Word final" was not so clear, though I judged—and I think rightly—that it meant that the word "final" was to be used as a password by which the two messengers should know each other.

I was almost at my destination, and was cogitating the message and its meaning, when the cab checked at some traffic in Barbican, just by the "Compasses" public-house, and Mr. Victor Peytral hailed me and climbed on the step of the cab.

"I was just going to see if Mr. Hewitt was at the place," he said, "and if so to ask him for news. But I am rather in a hurry, and perhaps you can tell me?"

"We are on the track, I think," I answered, "and I have just come across this, which I am taking to Hewitt," and with that I showed him my translation of the cypher, and gave him its history in half a dozen sentences.

"That's good," Peytral answered. "I don't know Channel Marsh, do you? But probably Mr. Hewitt does. I won't keep you any longer—I see you're hurrying. But I hope to see you again before long."

He dropped off the step and disappeared, and the cab went on round the corner by the "Compasses."

I found Hewitt and Plummer in the office where, on pretence of bookbindery, I had first seen Mayes face to face the day before. They were near the completion of their examination of this office and all its contents, and soon would begin as systematically on the premises behind. I gave Hewitt my copy of the cypher message, and my translation, with an exact account of how it had come into my possession.

Martin Hewitt studied the message for a minute or two, and then relapsed into grave thought. So he sat for some little time, while Plummer left the room by the window and descended the ladder to speak with his men on guard below.

Presently Hewitt looked up and said: "Brett, this message is most important—probably as important as you suppose it to be. But at the same time I believe you have made a great mistake about it."

"But I haven't misread it, have I? Is there any other way——"

"No, you haven't misread it; you've read every word as it was intended to be read. But it is a very different thing from what you suppose it to be."

"What is it, then?"

Martin Hewitt put the paper on the table and looked keenly in my face. "It is a trap," he said. "It is a trap to catch *me*—unless I flatter myself unduly."

I could not understand. "A trap?" I repeated. "But how?"

"Why should Mayes need to send his confederate instructions by written note? We know the nature of his hold over his subordinates, and we know that it means personal communication. Also, the cheque was in Mayes's own hands last night. More, Mayes knows very well that I have read that cypher—has known it for some time; otherwise how could we have discovered the bonds in the case of the Lever Key? Also, Mayes knows that we have his cheque-book and know his bank. Didn't I assure you we were watched last night? I believe he knows all we have done. In such circumstances he might risk his jackal's liberty by sending him on the desperate chance of cashing a cheque, but, knowing the risk, he would never have let him come with information on him. And least of all would he have let him come carrying a vital secret written in that very cypher which he knows I read many weeks ago. And then see how that message, instead of being concealed, was positively brought to your notice! That man Broady Sims is a cunning rascal, and the police know him of old as a skilful swindler and bill-forger. A man like that doesn't get rid of a compromising scrap of paper by trundling it out under your nose just at the moment he is arrested, when the attention of everybody is directed to him; no, he would wait his opportunity, and then he would probably slip it into his mouth and swallow it. As it is, he would seem to have succeeded in dropping this paper full in your sight, with an elaborate pretence of secrecy. Now this is what has been done, Brett. That man has been sent to cash a cheque, with very little hope of success, or none, because the first move that Mayes would anticipate on our part would be the watching for him and his cheques at the bank in Upper Holloway. If by any chance the cheques had been cashed, well and good, no harm would have been done, and then Mayes could have gone on to arrange for drawing the rest of his balance—could probably have quite safely come himself to draw it. But if on the other hand, as he fully anticipated, Sims was arrested, what then? Nothing was lost but a penny cheque-form, and even Sims—though Mayes would care nothing about that—could only be searched and then released, for the cheque was perfectly genuine, and there was no charge against him. But since he would certainly be searched, that cypher note was given him, with instructions to make a conspicuous show of attempting to get rid of it. Now that note was written in a cypher which Mayes knew was as plain as print—to whom? To *me*. I am on his trail, and this note is deliberately flung in my way, open as the day, but with every appearance of secrecy. I am his dangerous enemy, and he knows it—as he told you, in fact, yesterday. If he can clear me away, he can take breath and make himself safe. The purpose of this note is to induce me to go, alone, to this place on Channel Marsh to-night at twelve, in the hope of learning where to find Mayes. There I am to be got rid of—murdered in some way, for which preparation will be made. Mayes judges my character pretty well. He knows that, in such circumstances as he represents, Sims being kept away from his appointment, I should certainly go and take his place, and use his password, to learn what I could. And, Brett, *that is precisely what I shall do!*"

"What? You will go?" I exclaimed. "But you mustn't—the danger! We'd better both go together."

Hewitt smiled. "Why not forty of us?" he said. "No. Here is a chance of bagging our man, for, however I am to be arranged for—whether by shot, steel, or the tourniquet, I make no doubt it is Mayes himself who is to do it. You shall come, however, you and Plummer at least. But we will not go in a bunch—you shall follow me and watch, ready to help when needful. This Channel Marsh is an empty, dark space between two channels of the Lea. It is among the Hackney Marshes, lying between Stratford and Homerton, and I fancy there is a deserted house there, though I can't remember ever having seen it. Do you know it?"

"No; not in the least."

"Well, I must reconnoitre to-day, and that with a lot of care. I think I told you I was convinced of being watched, and that is a thing you can't prevent in a place like London, if it is skilfully done. Now, Brett, you have done very well this morning. If you want to be on the scene of action to-night at twelve, you must get leave from your editor, mustn't you? How's your wrist?"

It was still extremely stiff, and I told Hewitt that I doubted my ability to hold a pen for two or three days.

"Very well, then; get off and convey your excuses as soon as you please. I shall have a talk with Plummer, and then I shall take a few hours to myself, by myself, in somebody else's clothes. Be in your rooms all the evening, for you may expect a message."

IV

It was at a little past nine in the evening that I next saw Hewitt. He came into my rooms in an incongruous get-up. He wore corduroy trousers, a very dirty striped jersey, a particularly greasy old jacket, and a twisted neckcloth; but over all was an excellent overcoat, and on his head a tall hat of high polish.

"Brought to me by Kerrett," he said, in explanation of the hat and overcoat. "He's been waiting with them for a long time in a court by Milford Lane. A good hat and overcoat will cover anything, and I preferred to enter this building in my own character. I've been wearing that this afternoon," and he pulled out of his pocket an old peaked cap with ear-pieces tied over the top.

"You mustn't bring your best clothes," he went on, "or you'll spoil them scrambling about boats and groping in ditches. I have done my ditch-groping for the day, and I'm going to change. You had best be putting on older things while I get into newer."

"What sort of place is this Channel Marsh?" I asked.

"Well, I should think there must be a great many better places to spend a night in. It must be the dreariest, wettest flat within many miles of London, and I should like to see the portrait of the man who had the idea of building a house there. For a house there is, or rather the ruins of it—deserted for years, and half carried away by rats and people who wanted slates and firewood and water pipes."

"Is that the place where you intend waiting to-night?"

"It is. I haven't examined it nearly so closely as I should like, for fear of raising a scare. Channel Marsh is almost an island, with a narrow neck of an entrance at each end. A foot-track runs the whole length, and a person in the ruined house can easily see anybody entering the Marsh from either end. For that reason I reconnoitred from a boat—the boat you will go in to-night. I think it is the very dirtiest old tub I ever saw, so that it suited my rig out. I discovered it at a wharf some little way down the river, and I paid a shilling for the hire of it. Channel Marsh is banked a bit on one side, and I crept up under cover of the bank. I learned very little, beyond the general lie of the land, because I was so mighty cautious. I judged it better to be content with half an examination, rather than drive away the game. And even as it is I've an idea I have been seen. I lay up among some reeds till dark, but after that I am *sure* there was somebody on the Marsh—and skulking, too, like me. So after waiting and scouting for a little I gave it up and paddled quietly back."

"But look here, Hewitt," I said, "this seems a bit mad. Why go and risk yourself as you talk of doing? You believe Mayes will be there, at the ruin, or will come there at twelve. Very well, then, why can't the police send enough men to surround the place and capture him for certain?"

Hewitt smiled and shook his head. "My dear Brett," he said, "you haven't seen the place, and I have. It will be hard enough job for you and Plummer to get near the spot unobserved, guided by a man who knows every inch. A trampling crowd of policemen would have as much chance as a herd of elephants, and on such light nights as we are having now they would be seen a mile off. And who knows what scouts he may have out? No, as I say, it will be a great piece of luck if you get through unobserved as it is, and even now I'm not perfectly certain that I couldn't do best alone. However, arrangements are made now, and you are coming, three of you."

"Then what are the arrangements?" I asked.

"Just these. You are to leave here first. Make the best of your way to Mile End Gate, where an old inn stands in the middle of the road. Go to the corner of the turning opposite this, at the south side of the road. At eleven o'clock a four-wheeler will drive up, with Plummer and one of his men in it. The man is one who knows all the geography of Channel Marsh, and he also knows exactly where to find the boat I used to-day. You will drive to a little way beyond Bow Bridge, and then Plummer's man will lead you to the boat. You had better scull and leave the others to look out. They will know what to do. You will pull along to a place where you can watch till you see me coming on to the Marsh by the path. As soon as you see me you will slip quietly along to a place the policeman will show you, close to the ruin, and watch again. That's all. I don't know whether or not you think it worth while to take a pistol. I certainly shall; but then I'm most likely to want it. Plummer will have one."

I thought it well worth while, and I took my regulation "Webley"—a relic of my old Volunteer captaincy. Then, by way of the underground railway, I gained the neighbourhood of Mile End, and interested myself about its back streets till the time approached to look for Plummer's cab.

Plummer was more than punctual—indeed, he was two or three minutes before his time. The cab drew near the kerb and scarcely stopped, so quickly did I scramble in.

"Good," said Plummer; "we're well ahead of time. Mr. Hewitt quite right?"

"Yes," I said. "I left him so an hour and a half ago at his office." And we sat silent while the cab rattled and rumbled over the stony road to Bow Bridge, and the shopkeepers on the way put up their shutters and extinguished their lights.

Bow Bridge was reached and passed, and presently we stopped the cab and alighted. Here Styles, Plummer's man, took the lead, and a little way farther along the road we turned into a dark and muddy lane on the left. We floundered through this for some hundred and fifty yards or so, and then suddenly drew in at an opening on the right. Here we stood for a few moments while our guide groped his way down toward the muddy water we could smell, rather than see, a little way before us.

There were a few broken steps and a broad black thing which was the boat. We got into it as silently as we could manage, and cast off. It was a clumsy, broad-beamed, leaky old conveyance, and that it was as dirty as Hewitt had described it I could feel as I groped for the sculls and got them out. The night was light and dark by turns—changing with the clouds. We shipped the rudder, and Styles steered, or I should probably have run ashore more than once, for the banks were not always distinct, and the channel was narrow and dark. We passed the black forms of several factories with tall chimneys, and then drew out among the Marshes, flat and grey, with wisps of mist lying here and there. So we went in silence for a while, till at last we drew in against the bank on the left and laid hold by a post at a landing-place.

"This is the Channel Marsh," whispered Styles, as we climbed cautiously ashore. "We can't see the house very well from here, but there's where Mr. Hewitt will come through."

Looking over the top of the low bank, we could discern a path which traversed the length of the marsh, entering it by a broken gate at a neck of land which we must have passed on our way. Here we crouched and waited. We had heard the half-hour struck on some distant clock soon after entering the boat, and now we waited anxiously for the three-quarters. So long did the time seem to my excited perceptions that I had quite decided that the clock must have stopped, or, at any rate, did not chime quarters, when at last the strokes came, distant and plaintive, over the misty flats.

"A quarter of an hour," Plummer remarked. "He won't be a minute late, nor a minute too early, from what I know of him. How long will it take him from that gate to the ruin?"

"Eight or nine minutes, good," Styles answered.

"Then we shall see him in seven minutes or six minutes, as the case may be," Plummer rejoined in the same low tones.

Slowly the minutes dragged, with not a sound about us save the sucking and lapping of the muddy river and the occasional flop of a water-rat. The dark clouds were now fewer, and the moon was high and only partially obscured by the thinner clouds that traversed its face. More than once I fancied a sound from the direction of the ruin, and then I doubted my fancy; when at last there was a sound indeed, but from the opposite direction, and in a moment we saw Hewitt, muffled close about the neck, walking briskly up the path.

We regained the boat with all possible speed and silence, and I pulled my best, regardless of my stiff wrist. During our watch I had had time to perceive the wisdom of the arrangements which had been made. We had been watching from a place fairly out of sight from the ruin, yet sufficiently near it to be able to reach its neighbourhood before Hewitt; and certainly it was better to approach the actual spot at the same time as Hewitt himself, for then, if he were being watched for, the attention of the watcher would be diverted from us.

Presently we reached the reed-bed that Hewitt had spoken of, and I could see a sort of little creek or inlet. Here I ceased to pull, and Styles cautiously punted us into the creek with one of the sculls. The boat grounded noiselessly in the mud, and we crept ashore one at a time through mud and sedge.

The creek was edged with a bank of rough, broken ground, grown with coarse grass and bramble, and as we peeped over this bank the ruined house stood before us—so near as to startle me by its proximity. It must have been a large house originally—if, indeed, it was ever completed. Now it stood roofless, dismantled, and windowless, and in many places whole rods of brickwork had fallen and now littered the ground about. The black gap of the front door stood plain to see, with a short flight of broken steps before it, and by the side of these a thick timber shore supported the front wall. It struck me then that the ruin was perhaps largely due to a failure of the marshy foundation.

The place seemed silent and empty. Hewitt's footsteps were now plain to hear, and presently he appeared, walking briskly as before. He could not see us, and did not look for us, but made directly for the broken steps. He mounted these, paused on the topmost, and struck a match. It seemed a rather large hall, and I caught a momentary glimpse of bare rafters and plasterless wall. Then the match went out and Hewitt stepped within.

Almost on the instant there came a loud jar, and a noise of falling bricks; and then, in the same instant of time I heard a terrific crash, and saw Hewitt leap out at the front door—leap out, as it seemed, from a cloud of dust and splinters.

I sprang to my feet, but Plummer pulled me down again. "Steady!" he said, "lie low! He isn't hurt. Wait and see before we show ourselves."

It seemed that the floor above had fallen on the spot where Hewitt had been standing. He had alighted from his leap on hands and knees, but now stood facing the house, revolver in hand, watching.

There was a moment's pause, a sound of movement from the upper part of the ruin, another quiet moment, and then a bang and a flash from high on the wall to the right. Hewitt sprang to shelter behind the heavy shore, and another shot followed him, scoring a white line across the thick timber.

Plummer was up, and Styles and I were after him.

"There he is!" cried Plummer, "up on the coping!" I pulled out my own pistol.

"Don't shoot!" cried Hewitt. "We'll take him alive!"

Far to the right, on the topmost coping of the front wall, I could see a crouching figure. I saw it rise to its knees, and once more raise an arm to take aim at Hewitt; and then, with a sudden cry, another human figure appeared from behind the coping and sprang upon the first. There was a moment of struggle, and then the rotten coping crumbled, and down, down, came bricks and men together.

I sickened. I can only explain my feeling by saying that never before had I seen anything that seemed so long in falling as those two men. And then with a horrid crash they struck the broken ground, and the pistol fired again with the shock.

We reached them in a dozen strides, and turned them over, limp, oozing, and lifeless. And then we saw that one was Mayes, and the other—Victor Peytral!

We kept no silence now, but Plummer blew his whistle loud and long, and I fired my revolver into the air, chamber after chamber. Styles started off at a run along the path towards the town lights, to fetch what aid he might.

But even then we had doubt if any aid would avail Mayes. He was the under man in the fall, and he had dropped across a little heap of bricks. He now lay unconscious, breathing heavily, with a terrible wound at the back of the head, and Hewitt foretold—and rightly—that when the doctor did come he would find a broken spine. Peytral, on the other hand, though unconscious, showed no sign of injury, and just before the doctor came sighed heavily and turned on his side.

First there came policemen, and then in a little time a hastily dressed surgeon, and after him an ambulance. Mayes was carried off to hospital, but with a good deal of rubbing and a little brandy, Peytral came round well enough to be helped over the Marshes to a cab.

The trap which had been laid for Hewitt was simple, but terribly effective. The floor above the hall—loose and broken everywhere—was supported on rafters, and the rafters were crossed underneath and supported at the centre by a stout beam. The rafters had been sawn through at both ends, and the rotten floor had been piled high with broken brick and stone to a weight of a ton or more. The end of a loose beam had been wedged obliquely under the end of the one timber now supporting the whole weight, so that a pull on the opposite end of this long lever would force away the bricks on which the beam rested and let the whole weight fall. It was the jar of the beam and the fall of the first few loose bricks that had so far warned Hewitt as to enable him to leap from under the floor almost as it fell.

Peytral's sudden appearance, when we had time to reflect on it, gave us a suspicion as to some at least of the espionage to which Hewitt had been subjected—a suspicion confirmed, later, by Peytral himself after his recovery from the shock of the fall. For fresh news of his enemy had re-awakened all his passion, and since he alone could not find him, he was willing enough to let Hewitt do the tracking down, if only he himself might clutch Mayes's throat in the end. This explained the "business" that had called him away after the Barbican stronghold had been captured; finding both Hewitt and Plummer somewhat uncommunicative, and himself somewhat "out of it," he had drawn off, and had followed Hewitt's every movement, confident that he would be led to his old enemy at last. What I had told him of the cypher message had led him to hunt out Channel Marsh in the afternoon, and to return at midnight. He, of course, regarded the message, as I did myself at the time, as a perfectly genuine instruction from Mayes to Sims, and he came to the rendezvous wholly in ignorance as to what Hewitt was doing, and with no better hope than that he might hear something that would lead him in the direction of Mayes. He had entered the marsh after dark from the upper end, and had lain concealed by the other channel till near midnight; then he had crept to the rear of the ruin and climbed to where an opening seemed to offer a good chance of hearing what might pass in the hall. He had heard Hewitt approach from the front, and the crash that followed. The rest we had seen.

V

Mayes never recovered consciousness, and was dead when we visited the hospital the day after; both skull and spine were badly fractured. And the very last we saw of the Red Triangle was the implement with which it had been impressed, which was found in his pocket.

It was a small triangular prism of what I believe is called soapstone. It was perhaps four inches long, and the face at the end corresponded with the mark that Hewitt had seen on the forehead of Mr. Jacob Mason. It fitted closely in a leather case, in the end of which was a small, square metal box full of the red, greasy pigment with which the mark had been impressed.

It was from Broady Sims that we learnt the exact use and meaning of this implement: though he would not say a word till he had seen with his own eyes Mayes lying dead in the mortuary. Then he gasped his relief and said, "That's the end of something worse than slavery for me! I'll turn straight after this."

Sims's story was long, and it went over ground that concerns none of Hewitt's adventures. But what we learned from it was briefly this. It had been Mayes's way to meet clever criminals as they left gaol after a term of imprisonment. In this manner he had met Sims. He had made great promises, had spoken of great ideas which they could put into execution together, had lent him money, and then at last had "initiated" him, as he called it. He had put him to lie back in a chair and had directed his gaze on the Red Triangle held in the air before him: and then the Triangle had descended gently, and he felt sleepy, till at the cold touch of the thing on his forehead his senses had gone. This was done more than once, and in the end the victim found that Mayes had only to raise the Triangle before him to send him to sleep instantly. Then he found that he must do certain things, whether he wanted or not. And it ended in complete subservience; so that Mayes could set him to perpetrate a robbery and then appropriate the proceeds for himself, for by post-hypnotic suggestion he could force him to bring and hand over every penny. More, the poor wretch was held in constant terror, for he knew that his very life depended on the lift of his master's hand. He could be sent into lethargy by a gesture and killed in that state. That very thing was done, in fact, as we have seen, in two cases.

Sims was but one of a gang of such criminals, brought to heel and made victims. Their minds and souls, such as they were, had passed into the miscreant's keeping, and terror reinforced the power of hypnotism. They committed crimes, and when they failed they took the punishment; when they succeeded Mayes took the gains, or at any rate the greater part of them. He went, also, among people who were not yet criminals, and by degrees made them so, to his own profit. The case of Henning, the correspondence clerk, was one that had come under Hewitt's eyes. He used his faculty also with great cunning in other ways—as we had seen in the matter of the Admiralty code. And it was even said among the gang that a man he had once hypnotised he could force by suggestion to commit suicide when he became useless or inconvenient.

Sims and the ragged fellow who had decoyed me into Mayes's den were the only members of the gang whom we could identify after his death, but many others must have shared their relief; and I sincerely hope—though I hardly expect—that they all availed themselves of their liberty to abandon their evil courses. As in fact the two I speak of did, and took to honest work.

All that had remained mysterious in the earlier cases now became clear. In the first, the case of Samuel's diamonds, Denson had been put into the office where Samuel had found him, by Mayes, with the express design of effecting a diamond robbery. The robbery was effected, and the unhappy Denson formed a plan of making a bolt of it himself with the diamonds. He was, perhaps, what is called a difficult subject in hypnotism—amenable enough to direct influence, but not sufficiently retentive of post-hypnotic suggestion. He hid the jewels and adopted a disguise, but Mayes was watching him better than he supposed. The diamonds were lost, but Denson was found and done to death—probably not in that retreat near Barbican, but at night in some empty street. The diamonds were not found on him, and the body, with the mark of the Triangle still on it, was taken by night to a central spot in London and there left. Mayes probably thought that a notable example like this, so boldly displayed and so conspicuously reported in the Press, would impress his auxiliaries throughout London with the terror that was one of his weapons; for they would well understand the meaning of the Red Triangle, and they would receive a striking illustration of the consequences of rebellion or bad faith. The money and the watch were left in the pockets because they were trifles after the loss of fifteen thousand pounds' worth of diamonds, and their presence in the pockets made the murder the less easy to understand—which was a point gained. And as to the keys—Mayes knew nothing of where the diamonds were hidden, and so had no use for them. For where could he use them? Denson had left his lodgings, and as to the office, that, he would guess, would be in the hands of the police, on Samuel's complaint. The immediate result of this affair on the only honest member of Mayes's circle I have told in the case of Mr. Jacob Mason. He was not yet thoroughly in Mayes's hands, but he had "dabbled," as he remorsefully confessed, and Mayes had already found him useful. He was dangerous, and his end came quickly. Another victim who had probably begun innocently enough was Henning, the clerk to Kingsley, Bell and Dalton, and his death in the Penn's Meadow barn leaves a mystery that never can be positively cleared up. Was it murder or was it suicide by post-hypnotic suggestion? It will be remembered that the fire burst out in the barn after Mayes had left it.

The case of Mr. Telfer was explained clearly enough by Hewitt at the time; but it is an example of the snares that lie open for the most innocent person who allows himself to be made the subject of hypnotic experiments at the hands of persons with whom, and with whose objects, he is not thoroughly acquainted. And it must be remembered that at this time there are persons advertising to teach the practice of hypnotism to anybody who will pay; to anybody who may use the terrible power as he pleases. More, the danger is so great that it has led two eminent men of science to issue a public protest and warning, with an urgent plea that the practice of hypnotism be restricted by law at least as closely as that of vivisection.

As to what would have happened if Plummer and I had yielded to Mayes's threats so far as to undergo the "initiation" he proposed, at the time we were helpless in his hands—of that I have little doubt. I cannot suppose that he would have wasted much time over me, once I had fallen lethargic. When Hewitt burst in he would have found me lying dead, with the Red Triangle on my forehead. It would have saved Mayes a lot of noise and struggle, at least.

But I often wonder whether or not there was anything in his reference to the place beyond the sea, where he would make me a great man if I did as he wished. Was it his design, having accumulated sufficient wealth, to return and take his natural place among the enlightened rulers of Hayti? He would not have been so much worse than some of the others.

LaVergne, TN USA
24 March 2010
177053LV00005B/113/P